SHIFT CHANGE

Mark Hunter

Shift Change

Cover Art by fiverr.com/germancreative
Editing by DocEditing.com

CONTENTS

Prologue

One week ago, I was still somewhat gainfully employed at a gas station in the small college town of Mount Pleasant, Michigan. I had been working at that store for five years and for reasons that should become pretty clear, I felt that it was time to make a change. I had felt that way since my first week on the job but had wanted to make sure that I gave the position and place a real chance to grow on me. When it came to things that didn't come easily to me, I had always been a quitter and I sought to change that when I graduated from college and found my way to the store.

It was the late spring of 2001, the state's economy was in the toilet, and I was expected to be grateful for the chance to work in any full-time part-time position. I actually tried to force myself to buy into that type of thinking but ended up just pretending that there was a valid reason for standing still while the world passed me by. The truth of the matter was that I stayed at the store because it was convenient. It was easier to stay than it would have been to go. It was easier to tell myself that I needed something to bridge the gap between college and the real world. The reality was that I had never learned the difference between failing up and falling down. Both felt like failure to me, so I played it safe.

I wasn't willing to admit it then, but the state that I was in when I started my adult life was one entirely of my own making. While I had done exactly as expected of me and graduated with honors from Central Michigan University, I had never looked at college as if it were preparation for a career. In the beginning,

I'd listened to my parents and made sure to study the things that interested me. As the semesters passed, there seemed to be fewer and fewer classes capable of holding my attention. I was far more concerned with theoretically meeting girls and occasionally writing lousy poetry and half-heartedly running an independent record label than with legitimately planning for my future. I wanted to get out of college and start working a boring job that would pay enough to keep me afloat so that I could continue to tell myself I was moving toward my poorly thought-out and ill-defined goals. I felt that if I maintained low expectations in life, I was much less likely to be let down. I attended career counseling at the university and left with the confirmation that my aptitudes did not meet my interests. I was told that people with my personality type who looked for their perfect career tended to float from job to job their whole lives and that it would be best to pick a major and stick with it.

I had been a model student, but I never really learned how to do anything in school. I was a talented writer when it came to putting papers together, and gifted in the rote memorization of facts, but I never did develop skill or passion for my chosen major, broadcast and cinematic arts. I showed up early for my classes and took excellent notes, but I couldn't bring myself to get involved, make contacts or bother with trying to set myself up with an internship. The further that my studies took me away from five-paragraph essays, standardized tests, and credit for attendance and keeping my mouth shut, the more I struggled. When school started to resemble the real world, I stopped being able to coast through, and lost interest. I'd always heard that short of being a skilled tradesman, a bachelor's degree would be the bare-minimum requirement for a non-minimum-wage job. To escape that world and appease my parents, I stuck with the university and held on to the idea it would serve as a foot in the door, which was all I would ever need given my work ethic. I would have been better served by blazing through an associate degree program with my sights set on working in a secretarial role in an office or hospital, but I didn't know that at the time. I'll have to keep it in mind for the next go around.

People do many things in a lot of different ways for any number of reasons, but the common thread among them is that we default to whatever we find to be the easiest at the time. That is not to say that we're all incurably lazy or that we aren't all trying to do something great, but it does mean that we are hardwired to take the path of least resistance. It's no wonder. Evolutionarily, there is an excellent argument for trying to solve problems in the way that requires you to exert the least amount of energy. Given a full stomach and no clear and credible threats, a dog will happily spend the day snoozing on the couch with his belly exposed. As easy as it is to see this in the animal kingdom, there's a tendency for humans to say that we are somehow different. We're woefully unequipped with the ability to view our own actions objectively, and there's no way to change that. We spend our lives trying to do things in the way that comes most naturally rather than in the way that is likely to achieve the desired effect. We're so wrapped up in remaining comfortable and secure that we sacrifice both function and meaning. We're left with nothing—so we lie to ourselves and to one another in the precise way that is convenient at the moment. The narrative is always subject to change.

There are a lot of different ways to frame the story of your life. Commonly, people cast themselves as the hero and build up whatever minor obstacles might be faced into some sort of worthy adversary. Starting to think of your mundane tribulations as something akin to your own personal Vietnam is tempting. Once you've talked up the seriousness of the battles that you are fighting, you might oversimplify and tell yourself that they are the only roadblocks to your success. If you're a positive person, you'll look at these obstacles as things to conquer and you'll gain quite a bit of satisfaction over the smallest of victories, regardless of how much relevance they might have to the next stage. If you're a more cynical person, you will see the glass as completely empty and refuse to recognize the possibility of any progress. On the off chance that you're a well-adjusted person, you will see things for what they are and take on the heaviest burden you can bear and understand that each step is necessary if there is to be any hope for reaching the next. However, if you're like me, you are too busy trying to forget how you got so lost to pay attention to the rest of the trip, much less, your inevitable destination. Let me explain...

Chapter Zero

I should have known something was up when the person I spoke with would offer no details about what the job would actually entail, but that didn't stop me from showing up for the interview. I had been trying to find a job for over three months and had not received a single call back on any of my inquiries. When I followed up and asked if the positions were filled, I was predictably met with reactions ranging from indifference to annoyance. My last place of employment had been the Robinson Dining Commons on the university campus, where I had done part-time early-morning grilled-cheese sandwich-prep work for $5.90 per hour. Most of the jobs I had applied for since receiving my degree were comparable in duties and pay to that position, but this one was different. The advertisement in the *Morning Sun* had stated that there were twenty-five positions to fill and that it would pay 400 dollars per week; that was more than enough to pique my interest. I called to find out the location so I could come in and fill out an application and learned that the paperwork wouldn't be necessary until after the interview. From what I'd gathered, the job was an entry-level position that the company needed to fill as soon as possible. They seemed to be taking a sort of job fair approach to the hiring process, so I felt okay about my chances.

As I drove down Mission Street and looked for the address, it became more and more evident that the business was likely located within a strip mall. Based on the numbers, I deduced that it would be in the same plaza as the old Kmart. As I prepared to make a left turn into what had recently become an unnecessarily large parking lot, a white vinyl banner with navy blue lettering caught my eye. It was attached to the front of a building that housed one of the last non-buffet Chinese restaurants in town and the local branch office of the Secretary of State—what most other states correctly called the Department of Motor Vehicles. The banner was the sort that you might see over the entryway to a pop-up tax service or a Halloween store, but it wasn't the right season for either of those businesses. In the font I readily identified as Comic Sans, the banner read:

PREFERRED SYSTEMS, LLC.

The advertisement had said that the company was new to the area, and as such, I felt the quality of their signage was forgivable. The desperation in the advertisement had appealed to me and I had assumed that I would not be required to sell myself too much, but I was still nervous when I got out of my car. I had no idea what was going to be asked of me and I no way of knowing whether I would be capable of doing it and I could already feel the imposter syndrome setting in. I caught a glimpse of myself in the glass door before I walked in and confirmed that I still looked like an idiot with my shaved head and baby face and oversized button-down dress shirt tucked into the black slacks that hadn't fit me since my senior year of high school. I hadn't known how I should dress, and that was the best that I could do; I knew that it wasn't going to be good enough. I would rather have prepared grilled cheese sandwiches for the rest of my life than try to survive a single interview, but I hadn't been getting any callbacks from the cafeteria, either. I took a deep breath and opened the door.

When I entered the building, a standing sign pointed me toward the area where interviews would be taking place. I walked through a sparsely decorated room that featured nothing more than a few empty desks and a poorly drawn chart on a dry-erase board. I had only started making sense of the chicken-scratch when a nondescript woman ushered me into another room of identical shape and size. This room was completely empty except for a circle of fifteen to twenty folding chairs. I picked a random chair and had a seat, hoping beyond hope that I wouldn't have to take part in any sort of group introduction. I was ten minutes early, and I assumed that the interviewer was finishing up with another prospective employee. After five minutes of waiting for something to happen, more applicants began to trickle in and sit in the other chairs. They ranged from businessmen in cheap suits to young guys straight from the frat house to the average forty-year-old hairdresser, and none of them seemed to know each other. Still, I heard chatter begin to pick up, centering around the unknown specifics of the job for which we had all answered the advertisement.

It was only when the seats were filled that a Preferred Systems employee came into the room. He was a white guy with an orange tan and a bleached smile, and I judged him to be in his early forties. He had frosted tips and was carrying too much weight around the midsection to be wearing a shirt with such a tight fit, and he was bursting with nervous energy. He looked like the sort of person who was going to try to sell you something and would follow you all the way back to your car, refusing to take no for an answer even as you drove away. The idea that he was recruiting us for work in a call center crossed my mind, and I hoped that we wouldn't be expected to do any sales if that was the case because I couldn't see myself making a single cold call. The group's side conversations continued until our host finally decided that ten minutes after the time of the appointment would be the cut-off.

He took a deep breath, tucked his baby-blue polo into his khaki shorts, and clapped his hands together before looking straight at me and instructing, "Grab that door, Yakob."

As I was still feeling self-conscious about the way I had dressed, I immediately knew that he was trying to make a Church of Mormon joke. He had failed, but his attempt was met with enough laughter so that he seemed satisfied that he had begun establishing rapport. I felt the blood rush to my face, and I was flushed with the sort of anger that had defined much of my experience with men throughout my twenty-one years. For whatever reason, I had never learned how to take a joke. Any attempt that I had ever made at "playing the dozens" or giving better than I got was always met with confusion and laughter at the nature of my joke or, in some cases, the sort of teasing that moved past supposed good-natured ribbing. Whenever I tried to defend myself and play the little dominance game, I tended to either miss my spots or hit back too hard. In this instance, I decided to hold my tongue. After all, I would still have been ostensibly trying to walk out of the building having secured employment.

"Alright, everybody. Listen up. I'm going to tell you all a little about myself. After that, you're going to tell us all a little about you. My name is John Adduci. I was born and raised about five miles up the road in Rosebush. Rosebush High School, class of 1995. Anybody else here from Rosebush? Raise your hands!"

John's query wasn't met with the sort of fanfare that he seemed to imagine it would be, but he seemed unfazed. As for me, I was busy thinking about what he might have been doing to have aged so poorly. I had received my own diploma in 1997.

"Like a lot of you, I went straight from Rosebush High to Mid Michigan Community College. First person in my family to go to college. I'm not saying that I was a good student, but I tried hard, and two good things came out of my two years in school. One, I got myself an associate degree in business administration and two, I met a smokin' hot girl there."

This planned pause resulted in a few chuckles, which seemed to give old Johnny a little more pep. He started pacing around the circle, making quick eye contact, and began emphasizing his speech with some of the most cliché hand gestures ever imagined. I looked around the circle and noticed that some people seemed wholly transfixed by his performance, while others couldn't be bothered to pretend to pay attention. He continued to speak.

"So, we both finished up there, and a couple of things happened. One good, and one not so good. One, my girl got pregnant. And the good thing... Nah, seriously," he said, met with muffled groans from his captive audience.

"Seriously, here—one, I got my girl pregnant and two, I couldn't find a job. I did everything right, man. I treated my job search like it *was* my job. Forty hours a week. I took all the interviews I could and man, nothing was below me. I knew that I was gonna have another mouth to feed and I knew that I had responsibilities; I knew that I had a family. I knew that I had to do what a man's gotta do."

He took a deep breath, likely kicking himself for not having broken out his best John Wayne.

"I ended up at a McDonalds, asking people if they wanted fries with that for five fifteen an hour, man. I kept taking interviews in the afternoon after working the early shift, changing into my good clothes, and showing up at nice places smelling like a McNugget. It was humbling, man. No one was biting, and I started to wonder why I even took out those student loans in the first place. My girl stopped working a month before her due date, and things got rough. Most of my check was going to insurance. We was po'," he said, pausing and looking around the room.

"You know why they call broke people po'?"

No one answered.

"Because they can't afford the O-R," he said, laughing heartily at his own joke before stopping and putting on a more serious face.

"That baby came, and we couldn't afford that operating room. Oh, they still let us use it, though, man. They just sent the bills. And the bills, they just kept coming. That's what they did. They kept coming and things got bad, and things got worse. In fact, they kept getting worse until one day, I answered an ad in the paper. What ad you think I answered?"

The hairdresser raised her hand.

"Shit, this ain't school, you can just talk," said John.

"Preferred Systems," said the hairdresser.

"Preferred Systems is right," said John.

"Now, how many of you here ever took home one thousand dollars in one week? Some of you? I bet you didn't do it for too long, did you? Nah, that never lasts. That never lasts when they're deciding what you get paid. But what if you got to have a say in how much they paid you?"

It was at that point I heard a dismissive voice call out from the back of the room.

"It's Kirby, everybody."

"It's who?" said John, annoyed that the cat had been let out of the bag.

Most of the people started getting up from their chairs and filed out in a demonstration of their shared disgust. For his part, John didn't seem all that surprised to see his audience dwindle. He paced a bit and began to move some chairs to the back of the room as he waited for the commotion to die down. When he appeared satisfied that there would be no more deserters, he spoke to the four of us still there.

"Look, people—I won't bullshit you. It's Kirby. We sell a professional-quality carpet cleaning system, door to door, and we do it well. We make real good money, and we'll show you exactly how we do it. You make your own hours, you call the shots, but you get paid on commission. If you don't think you can do that, this ain't the place for you. But if you believe in yourself, then you can come back tomorrow at the same time, and we'll get you started. Deal?"

Needless to say, I wasn't qualified to come back. The number of lower-end BMW and Mercedes vehicles in the parking lot definitely suggested that there was money in hawking vacuum cleaners, but I knew that I wasn't going to be the one to make it. I needed something stable, with an income that I could depend upon. The money that I might make chasing leads and channeling my desperation into a sales pitch would be anything but guaranteed. If I had the sort of confidence that might have led me to become a good pitchman, I would not have been answering vague help-wanted ads less than three months after receiving a bachelor's degree. If I had been that sort of person, I would have spent more time in college learning my craft and preparing to enter the workforce rather than trying to graduate with the least amount of credits necessary so as not to waste any more of my family's money. With no prospects, no plan, and no returned calls, I finally made the decision to call a temporary employment agency.

CONVENIENCE

Chapter One

It's an unfortunate reality for most of us that our passions rarely match up with our abilities. In the rare case that they do, it is worth noting that having a talent for something is nothing if one doesn't understand how much work is required to turn it into a successful career. We've already established my interests—writing about myself, listening to indie rock music, and obsessing over cute girls—but we haven't touched much on my abilities. Simply put, my skills never had much of anything to do with the things that I cared about. I cracked the formula to getting good grades on creative writing projects in high school, only to be stared at blankly by Professor Herb Scott of Western Michigan University when I submitted my first batch of terrible poems. I worked hard to become a veritable encyclopedia of underground music knowledge, but I never could figure out how to write a melody one quarter-note as good as the ones that my friends threw away on a regular basis. As for women—well, I had established an unblemished record of being the sort of really good friend that no girl would ever dream of taking the chance of losing. For all my rebel posturing, it was clear early on that my best bet would be to find the part of the machine that most needed the sort of cog that I was most suited to become. I resisted for way too long, and I was out of college by the time I came to my senses. By then, I think it was already far too late.

***

"Good morning, and it's a great day at Advance Employment. This is Justin, how can I help you?"

I never did hear Justin answer the phone any other way during the six months that I worked for that company. On the first call, he walked me through a short screening process and invited me to come into the office to continue the interview, somehow managing to sound both cheerful and robotic. He asked me about my previous employment, education level and references and even though he placed me on hold several times over the course of a thirty-minute call, he didn't seem to miss a step during the whole conversation. It was impressive, entertaining, and more than a little off-putting. I couldn't help thinking about the way people tell children that they can be anything that they want to be and how damaging that advice can actually be. As far as I could tell, Justin had the title of administrative assistant coded straight into his DNA, and it would have been a disservice to the world for him to have been encouraged to do anything but answer phones and file paperwork for the rest of his life. By the time I hung up the phone, he had set up my interview with a specialist whose name sounded like it might have better suited a character from a Frank Zappa song.

Advance Employment Services was, like many of the businesses in Mount Pleasant, headquartered in a strip mall on Mission Street. It was located in the sort of building that might house the offices of various doctors of differing specialties, but the other commercial spaces were unoccupied. As a result of the proliferation of franchised eye doctor and dental care offices in the newer parts of town, it was clear that the empty storefronts would likely remain vacant for the foreseeable future. With college students home for the summer, the vast majority of the money spent in the local economy would now be focused on the restaurants and hotels near the casino on the northeast side of town. As for me, I was holding out hope that Buffy would be able to find me a stable position into which I might be hired as a full-time employee. Advance Employment Services staffed several local offices and factories, and as such, I was excited for a seemingly inevitable bump in pay from the $5.90 hourly wage that I had built up to over the years at the nearby college cafeteria.

When I arrived for my interview the next day, Justin greeted me at the front desk with the same rehearsed salutation that I had heard on the phone. While I'm not a verbal learner and I often have trouble making sense of a basic conversation, I immediately noticed that he used the exact same vocal inflection in person. He was a tall and clean-cut white man in his late twenties who appeared to be very tightly wound, and I instantly related to him when I saw how focused he was on the task at hand. He was neck deep in paperwork, and while he was the initial point of contact for both clients and customers of Advance Employment Services, it was clear that he couldn't have cared less about whoever may have walked in to disturb his process. He never looked up at me, but he did say my name and the time of my appointment before pointing the way to Buffy's office.

I didn't like Justin, but I didn't like myself very much at the time either, though, so it makes sense that I would feel a kinship with him. Dealing with people like him made it very tough for me to continue to tell myself that I was a likable person and it put the onus on me to work on myself. I didn't like that at all.

Logic Oil Company owned and operated approximately two dozen stores throughout Mid Michigan, including the home office located right there in Mount Pleasant. The company's convenience stores sold Shell petroleum products, and they dominated the local market. When I had first started looking for a full-time job towards the end of my final semester, I had set my sights on their High Street location for its sheer proximity to my apartment, but my calls were never returned. If I wasn't able to get in at that store, I had hoped that I would luck into a position at one of the other two locations located off Mission Street. The company's flagship store on Pickard Street was on the other side of town, and I wasn't excited at the prospect of making the three-mile walk every day when my transportation inevitably failed. After graduation, I had moved outside of town—far enough out that the Pickard Street Shell actually ended up as the closest Logic store. When I'd met with Buffy the specialist, I was assigned to work as a first shift cashier at that very station—now a five-mile trip on the Shoelace Express.

When I arrived for my initial meeting with the store manager, an older cashier offered me an abbreviated greeting in an unplaceable semi-southern drawl. She had a line of customers at the register, so her utterances were choppy, but she did point me down the hallway past the counter. After a few steps, I noticed that the sign for the ladies' room was straight in front of me and deduced that my new coworker's attempt at clairvoyance had failed. However, the first door on the right-hand side of the hallway was open. As no one was present in the room and there was quite a bit of barely concealed cash stacked on the desk, I chose not to enter. I took a quick glance around, noting the recent use of a vintage dot matrix printer and a Gateway personal computer that appeared to have shipped with Windows '95 as its standard operating system. I shifted my focus to look at some of the other antique equipment including an ancient, professional-grade videocassette recorder attached to a thick, monochrome monitor displaying a four-quadrant view of the store's security cameras. I had just noted that only three of the cameras were active when I heard my name called behind me in a strange sort of low, croaking voice.

"Jim, right?"

I didn't have any more friends left in town, so I was a bit thrown off as I turned around to see who had recognized me from the back of my head. It made much more sense when I saw that the person who had called my name was wearing a Shell polo shirt. When the man extended his hand and introduced himself, I noticed that he had a very soft handshake. I didn't have a firm handshake myself, and it always threw me off when a guy who wasn't obviously artsy or well-to-do had a similarly weak grip.

"Hey, Jim. I'm Paul. When can you start?"

When I met Paul Jackson, Store Manager of Logic Oil #106, he reminded me of most of the other guys I had met that were from the area. He was around thirty years old and wore more gold jewelry than you might expect for someone that drove a rusted-out red pickup truck. He was tall and thin, and his voice seemed to be more ravaged by cigarettes than it should have been for his years. Like many lower-middle-class white men at that place and time, he appeared to be practicing a sort of dual idolatry of both whitewashed urban culture and a modern cowboy sensibility that was all hat and no cattle. He smelled like stale cigarettes and lousy cologne, and I immediately hoped that he wouldn't transfer his stench to me. Despite his questionable life choices, he definitely appeared more intelligent than the average citizen. When I later learned that he lived in the tiny mobile home park at the back of the McDonalds next to the station, it made perfect sense that he would have been selected for the position. In theory, if needed, he could be at the station in less than thirty seconds.

"I have nothing going on. I could start now if you wanted, heh. I could start tomorrow morning, if that would be better," I said, eager to let Paul know that I was ready to be a team player. I needed money, and I needed it yesterday.

"Well, we need you for first shift, so how about tonight at ten?"

I was a bit confused, but I could see the merit in what would seem to be a stress-free overnight training session.

"Yeah, I can do that."

"You could also start tomorrow night if you want to try to figure out your sleep schedule."

Paul sensed my confusion and he spoke again. "Oh, shit, yeah. You probably didn't know that it was third shift."

"Well, I was told first shift," I said.

"Yeah, it's called first shift, but it's third shift. It's nights. We lost both our night guys, and my assistant manager has been working seven nights a week. Do you still want it? I mean, Advance will pay you seventy-five cents more an hour. It stays pretty busy overnight—not like days, but still busy—and there's a lot of cleaning but the hours are there for the taking if you want them."

I thought hard about it for just over five seconds and concluded that working overnight would suit me much more than working during the day. It sounded like I'd pretty much be left to my own devices and I would be able to listen to music and comedy and thus the nights would fly by. Besides the janitorial duties, I figured that there would be a fair amount of stocking to do, with a minimum of customer interaction. I could continue looking for a better job when I wasn't sleeping, and best of all, the money would be guaranteed. Buffy had assured me that Advance didn't operate like the standard agency; that is, they wouldn't be taking any money out of my checks. I was especially grateful for that, because while I would be working at least thirty-two hours per week, that first shift bonus would only push me to $5.90 per hour. Minimum wage wasn't what my parents had in mind for my first job out of college, but I had no confidence that I could do anything more involved than take notes and show up for class. There were no more notes to take and no more classes to attend, so I told Paul that I could start that night. He declined my offer, laughed, and told me to come back the following evening.

Chapter Two

People have always seemed to go out of their way to make their lives more difficult than they needed to be. By the time I was in high school, I understood that the distance between needs and wants was much greater than most of my peers imagined. I never had any delusions of grandeur or even illusions of competency. I never honestly thought that I was going to be a great writer or run a cool record label or anything that noteworthy. I always knew that my best path in life was going to be to shut up, follow the rules, get a degree and try to get a job in an office and be happy with that. The things that interested me would be best addressed on the side. I felt that as long as I kept my head down and didn't strive for much more than what being an honest person would provide me, I could expect to have a relatively fulfilling life. I had no interest in luxuries like nice cars, smiling children, a big house, a beautiful lawn, or even yearly vacations. I dreamed of things like paying bills, going to concerts, and being able to talk to women without second guessing every syllable that came out of my mouth. I didn't believe in a higher power, but I had this idea that the less I demanded out of life, the more likely I was to get what I did want.

***

As a first shift cashier, my shift began at ten in the evening and ended at six thirty in the morning. To encourage better communication between shifts, the beginning of my workday overlapped with the last half hour of third shift, and the end did the same with the first thirty minutes of second shift. Because

Logic had decided to refer to the night shift as first shift, this had created many misunderstandings over the years, but I learned it was apparently never suggested that things be changed to match the more familiar nomenclature. While intended to do the opposite, the posted schedule's curved line indicating the crossover from the previous day contributed to the confusion. This became most apparent when a team member would offer to cover a shift for a night cashier, only to fail to show up for the shift in question. This situation arose so many times that it was conveniently impossible to tell the difference between those who were legitimately crossed up and those who were using the strange schedule as an excuse.

When I arrived for my first shift, on the evening of Tuesday, May 8, 2001, the cashier on duty directed me toward the back room. As became customary, I was about a half an hour early for my shift. While there was a chair pushed underneath the cheap desk near the old-style punch clock, I found myself too nervous to sit. From a cursory glance, it was clear that the back area served as both the stock room and the break room. It was filthy, but the layers of grease and dirt found on the floors and walls weren't the sort that one could actually clean by any normal means, so it was partially understandable. The best that you could say about the room was that the cleaning supplies were one shelf closer to the rotting floor than the packaged food. The smell of mildew and mold permeated the air, and one glance at the stopped-up basin of the mop closet told me all that I needed to know. The entire building was badly in need of a good razing, but the non-customer-facing portion of the business was the least of the company office's concerns. It wasn't as if the store could ever have attracted more traffic— there was no justification for the company to spend any money on renovations.

"Come on bitch, where you at?"

I peeked out from the back room and saw the cashier leave her position behind the counter and head to the front door. She grabbed a lighter from a display and took out a pack of Newports from the pocket of her cheap dress pants. She sighed, lit her cigarette, and took her first drag before opening the door, surveying the parking lot, and finally settling in to enjoy her smoke. She spoke again.

"This is bullshit."

I hadn't paid attention to the person behind the counter when I'd entered the store, but the small scene that she had made allowed me the opportunity to get a sense of what she was all about. I guessed that she couldn't have been more than nineteen years old. She had long and straight blonde hair, she was rail thin, and she was apparently under the impression that she had grown up black. While the store manager may have dressed the part of the white-bread gangster, this girl seemed to have set her sights on being an undercover hood rat in a town without a hood. I had come across people like her in the past, but mainly through exposure to the early cinematic works of Harmony Korine. I wondered if she might have a tether curfew fast approaching or if she was a method actor doing some immersion work in preparation for an audition for the upcoming reboot of *COPS*. As I think back on it, both were possible.

"My old man is gonna be pissed," she said.

There were a few different people to which she may have been referring, and it had always been my policy not to ask people to explain themselves. I didn't like to encourage any interaction beyond what was necessary, and I always found it more worthwhile to just wonder rather than to get the actual answer in these situations. If she had been a young guy, she would most likely have been talking about her father. She wasn't overly feminine, and so that usage couldn't be immediately ruled out. Up to that point in my life, I had mainly heard middle-aged lower-middle-class white men refer to their wives as their 'old ladies.' I considered that she could be talking about her husband, but it seemed like a strange way to speak when she was likely not even out of her teens. As she finished sucking down her cigarette, the situation satisfied my idle curiosity.

"There he is," she said, ashing out the object of her addiction on the concrete ledge designated for that purpose.

I watched her walk out to meet a red Chevrolet Monte Carlo as it sped into the parking lot. When the car came to a stop, she leaned through the passenger side window and held a brief conversation with the driver before sealing it with a kiss. She headed back to the store.

"He hates taking care of the kid."

The old man, in fact, was an old man. An older man, anyway. He was an underweight white guy who looked to be in his late thirties, but it was hard to be sure of his age without being able to see his eyes. He wore Aviators and had excellent taste in ugly vehicles and some sort of lingering crush on the late Dale Earnhardt. He had to be twenty years older than my coworker, but the length of the kiss told me that he probably wasn't her father or even her older brother. Whether he was the father of the child he was tasked with looking after was not clear at that point, but I couldn't rule it out because plenty of parents can't stand dealing with their kids. The whole thing was a mess, so it all made perfect sense to me.

As we turned to enter the station, I decided to make an effort to learn my coworker's name through a quick glance at her name tag. The tattered badge pinned to her Shell polo shirt and held together with Scotch tape announced her name with a handwritten scrap of paper that read, "Crystal B."

"Yours is on the till, but you have to cut your name out and put it in," she said.

"Alright," I replied, as we entered the store.

The sight of a woman who appeared to be my trainer—judging by the fact that she was wearing a shirt matching the one Paul wore during my interview—greeted me. She was short and round with dyed auburn hair and the sort of long-term breathing issues that became apparent within ten seconds of my awareness of her existence. I had no idea how old she might be, but it was safe to say that she wasn't holding up well. It was approximately ten minutes after the beginning of the shift, and my trainer was leisurely preparing a cup of coffee that contained more cream and sugar than actual java. She seemed to be moving in slow motion, but by the end of the week, I would understand that she had actually been operating at what constituted a breakneck pace. She began speaking, although she hadn't yet turned around or made any sort of eye contact.

"Is it Jim or James?"

"Ah... um... I guess James since I'm at work."

"What do you prefer to be called, though?"

"His nametag says 'Jim,'" said Crystal.

"I guess it's Jim, then," I agreed.

"Well if you wanna be fancy, we can print a new one for you," said the unnamed woman.

"No, it's fine; my name is Jim, but most people call me—"

"Jim. Alright, fine. Hello, Jim Sims. I'm Donna."

"Hi," I replied, already uncomfortable. I was still unable to get over the whole rhyming thing.

"I'm Crystal, but you know that," said Crystal.

"Her name tag says Crystal B because when she started, there was another one," added Donna.

When we went to the back room to punch in for the shift, Donna remarked that she would have to go into the office to find me a blank timecard. I heard her rummaging around the office for about five minutes, after which she returned with a small notepad rather than an actual card. She remarked that she had been unable to locate one, and instead instructed me to write my name, the date, and the current time. I glanced at her timecard in the wall rack and saw that she had actually punched in before making her diabolical diabetic brew, but I did as she'd directed. She told me that I was welcome to clock in five minutes early if there were customers in the store upon my arrival and then invited me to help myself to coffee or a fountain drink, as they were free while we were on the clock. As I prepared the first of many cups of Diet Mountain Dew, I saw Crystal flash me a dirty look. Donna caught her in the act and told her that she was going to walk me through shift change and that we'd get her out of there as soon as we could. I shivered, as I had never found the Mother Bear persona the least bit endearing. I had no interest in being anyone's cub.

Once I clocked in, the first thing I learned to do was count the till. On top of the closed register's keypad, there was a fully loaded clipboard. I was to fill in my name, the date and the appropriate shift on the indicated lines on the top page, which was used to make a record of the money in the safe and register. I learned there should be five tens, ten fives, and fifty one-dollar bills—the ones paperclipped in two stacks of twenty-five. While the bills were separated by denomination, I was told not to trust that any bundles contained the proper number. As for the change, there should be a ten-dollar roll of quarters, a five-dollar roll of dimes, a two-dollar roll of nickels, and two fifty-cent rolls of pennies. Stray coins, such as silver or gold dollars were kept in their own compartment to the left of the quarters.

Donna encouraged me to add up my drawer with a nearby calculator when I finished counting, but I had been doing the math in my head as I went along. I decided to humor her and use the bulky and unfamiliar adding-machine as long as she was watching.

After writing the sum on the designated line of the sheet, I was to compare my total with the final number on the attached paperwork of the last person on my register. In this case, the totals matched up perfectly. Donna told me that if they were off, I would seek the assistance of the cashier that I was relieving to introduce a tiebreaker into the equation. If there was more money in the till than first documented, I would put the difference into a small manila envelope, numbered by shift, and drop it into the safe. If I worked a different shift, this process was not necessary, as the final numbers sent to the office were based on the overages and shortages of the business day. In the interest of brevity and not bringing undue suspicion onto myself, I decided that this would not be the best time to bring up the possibility of employees working together to undermine the other cashiers and the company. From what I had seen to that point, the staff was just as likely to have already carried out that scam as they were to have never thought about how easy that sort of thing might be. They didn't seem like the most trustworthy bunch, but they didn't seem like the most intelligent, either.

Once I counted and verified the till, I learned the proper way to read the cash controller safe. The safe held excess bills and change which were extracted as needed throughout the day. It contained plastic tubes filled with predetermined amounts of various denominations and was filled every morning by the manager or assistant manager. It featured a long piece of old masking tape placed above a series of holes used for front loading. This makeshift label featured faded guidelines for the amount of each type of currency to be loaded into each slot. When full, the safe contained a maximum of twelve dollars in pennies, twenty-four dollars in nickels, sixty dollars in dimes, one hundred twenty dollars in quarters, one hundred fifty dollars in ones, five hundred dollars in fives, and five hundred dollars in tens. It was read with the insertion of a brittle and duct-taped plastic measuring stick, using the depth to display the number of tubes left in each column in descending value. Donna once again encouraged me to use a calculator to total my findings, as the task required some basic multiplication.

"The cool thing about that safe is that it is timed so the most money a robber could get out of it would be one hundred dollars every two minutes," said Donna.

"So, what's the protocol when the robber gets angry that we can't give him the money faster?"

While Donna didn't seem to process my observation in the way I had intended, I did hear a dry laugh come from Crystal's direction. Donna continued.

"And even if you have a key like me, the robber would have to wait for ten minutes for the safe to open all the way. By then, you would have already taken the bills out of the thing in the register, and the cops would be on their way."

Chapter Three

When I was ten years old, I took the Stanford-Binet IQ test and scored somewhere in the high 140s, a number that has decreased with every subsequent test. I remember being proud of my results, but more than that, I remember my family's understandable confusion when it came to my early struggles in school. I showed quite a bit of promise in things like mental math and spelling and the memorization of various esoteric facts, but I was limited in my ability to relate to other children and play with them. I had severe problems focusing, and the truth is that I spent most of my time in my head. If I wasn't drawing intricately detailed but ultimately artless designs on blank sheets of paper, I was charting out the careers of fictitious baseball players. I was fascinated with numbers from an early age, but not in a way that would be applicable to real life. I liked memorizing the statistics of my favorite players and creating others in my head. I spent hours filling up college ruled notebooks with these otherwise indecipherable rows and columns of numbers, computing things like earned run average, total bases and on base percentage in my head. When I finished a page, I'd look back on the created player's career output with a sort of nostalgia for a monochrome world that never existed. I would take a glance at the final tallies and try to decide how realistic such a career would have been, and I'd conclude the session by balling up the paper and tossing it into the trash. It didn't take very long before I was only comfortable dreaming up journeymen and career minor-leaguers.

***

After comparing my safe total with Crystal's, Donna told me to switch to the second and final page of my paperwork. This sheet was dedicated entirely to the recording of the store's cigarette inventory. I later learned that most stations counted cigarettes only once a day and some even less than that, but Pickard Shell found it necessary to completely account for every pack in the store three times in a twenty-four-hour period. Management set up the sheet so that it resembled the racks and shelves in back of the counter, where the bulk of the cigarettes were kept. In addition to the blank spaces provided for the number of packs and cartons found in the individual rows, there were pre-tax prices and blank lines for the full cash value of the inventory on hand. There was plenty of math to be done, but my trainer told me that we would need to count the cartons first, with our initial focus on a cabinet with additional stock found in the back room. After we tallied the extra cartons, we'd count those in the front and then finally the single packs. Before completing the shift change, we would compare our counts against the ending tallies of the previous shift. There was a brief mention of a daily balancing sheet, but Donna told me that I was better off not asking questions about it at that juncture. She presented the process of the counting of the cigarettes as if it were a microcosm for humanity's shared existential struggle, and I couldn't help but be amused.

When we reached the back room, Donna opened the cabinet containing the cigarette overstock. It had four shelves, each of which looked to be holding between thirty and forty cartons at first glance. She explained which cartons belonged to which row on the sheet, according to their pre-tax prices. We carried brands ranging from the lower-end USA Golds to the higher-priced Camel Non-Filters to everything in between, but there were only four different pre-tax prices to memorize. Some brands were 'regular' brands, while others were considered 'premium' and still others were considered 'generic.' As Donna explained the groupings, I found myself more focused on the number of rows and columns of cartons found on each level. When she finished telling me which brands belonged to which pricing tier, she told me that she was going to call out the numbers and that I should write them down as she went. I watched her touch each carton with a pencil, counting out the numbers until she finished each shelf before beginning the next. I allowed her to continue running through her routine, but I went ahead and wrote down the totals that I had already reached through more basic multiplication. She lost count and started over several times throughout the task.

When we headed back out to the front of the store, I was surprised to see that business had picked up while we were counting cartons. There was a line of five or six customers, cars at several of the gas pumps, and the register was making a few different beeping noises. I made eye contact with an older gentleman near the back of the line and I could immediately sense his impatience, most likely related to the fact that three cashiers were working and only one of them was performing anything that could be even remotely be considered an act of customer service. Although things had gotten a bit hectic, I noted that Crystal didn't seem fazed by the situation. She had her head on a swivel as she watched the pumps, but she found the time to joke around and make small talk with the customers, whether interested or not. It was actually rather impressive. It was at that point that it occurred to me that there might be more to the job than I had first thought. Luckily for my financial state, Donna interrupted my train of thought before I managed to talk myself out of coming back for my second day.

After counting the cartons, we moved along to the individual packs of cigarettes. While the various brands shared space on the shelves, they were broken up by price point and marked by small scraps of paper featuring both a number and running tally of packs sold since the last count. Donna instructed me to count the packs one by one and compare them with Crystal's numbers. If I came up with a different number than she had for each section, I was to have her recount them and we would use whichever we both agreed on. If she were to get a third number, then we were to proceed until we came to the same conclusion. I considered bringing up the possibility that people might agree on the wrong number, but I thought better of it in the interest of trying to get Crystal out the door. As ready as she was to clock out for the night, she was actually still finishing up counting some packs of USA Golds that sat on a rack underneath the front counter. I heard her counting, one by one, at the precise time that I realized that each row could hold thirteen soft packs or twelve hard packs of cigarettes. I took to multiplying rows by twelves and thirteens whenever possible and adding by threes and subtracting remainders when necessary.

When we had agreed on the number of packs in each row, Donna showed me how to take inventory of the scratch-off lottery tickets. Much like the cigarettes, they were written down at the beginning and end of every shift. We carried sixteen tickets at a time, with prices ranging from one to twenty dollars. Each had a three-digit identifier that denoted what number it was in that particular bundle, with the one-dollar scratch-offs coming in packets of 250 and the twenty-dollar variety coming in a set matching their value. The tickets were to be loaded into the dispenser so that the first ticket sold numbered '000.' As I finished writing down my numbers, I noticed that several of the tickets appeared to be loaded backward. I had brought that up to Donna and started to compare my numbers with those found on Crystal's sheet when a customer leaned across the counter and pointed in the general direction of the ticket dispenser. The woman sported a mullet and was clad in an oversized blue T-shirt featuring a cartoon image of the Tasmanian Devil, with the whole outfit pulled together by the presence of some solid grey sweat shorts and a dirty pair of Crocs.

"Gimme a couple of those Cash For Alls," said the woman, without a hint of politeness.

I watched Crystal grab three two-dollar Cashword tickets and begin to erase the ending number on the corresponding line of her sheet.

"Anything else?"

"You better go ahead and pick one for me."

"One two-dollar ticket?"

"One *dollar* ticket. I can't spend that much."

I saw Crystal reach for one of the three one-dollar tickets and begin to tear it from the bundle at the perforation, only to hear the customer interrupt.

"But not that one. One of them Cash Pigs, there."

There was no Cash Pig ticket. There was a Cash Cow, which was the one that Crystal had attempted to select for the customer. Of course, there wasn't a Cash For All ticket either, but apparently, the Cashword had sufficed.

"Sorry, we just have the Cash Cow," said Crystal.

"Gold Rush," replied the customer.

"Fool's Gold?" asked Crystal, paperclipping the unsold Cash Cow ticket to the one hanging out of the dispenser.

"Yeah, that one."

"Anything else?"

"That's it," said the customer.

"Alright, it's going to be sev—"

"What number is them Wild Childs on?"

"Wild Time? The five-dollar or the two-dollar?" Crystal asked.

"No, Wild Child. The two-dollar."

"Sixty-six," said Crystal, who seemed to have given up on her attempts at correcting the woman.

"Oh lord… How about the five-dollar, then?"

"Five."

"Alright. Five on five. I better take five just to be sure," said the customer, impressed with her own turn of phrase.

"Alright… thirty-two dollars, sweetie."

The customer paid for the tickets and walked down the hallway to the Daily Lotto stand to scratch the tickets. She began talking to herself, peppering her language with a combination of folksy sayings and foul curse words. At the time, this was new to me, but I grew to understand that it was a common occurrence. As the customer continued her soliloquy, Crystal and I changed our respective numbers to match the new totals. We had just finished that process when a mustached man in a Carhartt jacket and dirty coveralls approached the counter and asked to buy the two tickets that our modern-day princess had decided against. Throughout his purchase, he joked with Donna in such a way that it made it very hard for Crystal to get through the transaction with any sort of efficiency. She eventually sold him the tickets, and he handed them back to her with a nod. She scratched away at the bottom of the tickets, revealed the appropriate code, and ran them each under the scanner in rapid succession. When the first ticket came back as a twenty-dollar winner and the Wild Time came back as a five, we saw the first customer poke her head around the corner with a look of disgust. She didn't stick around long enough to see the big winner give it all back and then some over his three trips to the station that evening, but if she had, she probably would have told him that it all had something to do with the number sixty-six.

Chapter Four

I wasn't raised to believe in God, but there was a short time in my childhood when the presence of a supreme being seemed like it should be a given. I never felt like the idea of a creator was realistic, but I do know that there were times that I wanted things so badly that I wanted to believe that there was someone to whom I could appeal when necessary. My strategy was never going to be to ask for riches or any incredible blessings but to only ask for little things, as I felt that I'd be more likely to receive them. From a young age, I never felt like I needed very much to be happy and so the few things that I held in high regard would theoretically be sure things should I send out a prayer. I started to doubt the existence of God when it became clear that my simple requests, such as an unexpected package of Reese's Peanut Butter Cups or for the Detroit Tigers to win the 1987 American League pennant, were not being granted. By the time I approached middle school, I spent most of my one-on-one time with God challenging him to prove his existence by making this or that girl smile at me during the bus ride home from school. It never happened, and I lost interest in the whole idea after that point.

***

After I verified that my numbers matched those of the previous shift and Donna had taken care of the night's first few customers, she excused herself. I heard her ask Crystal to "babysit" me while she used the restroom, as someone needed to make sure that my mere presence didn't result in any damage to the empty store. When the old man saw Crystal come out of the back room, he began laying on the horn of his car. It was immature, but I knew that it wasn't as if he didn't have a reason for getting frustrated at the situation. Crystal left the store in an attempt to calm him down and the register began a rhythmic pattern of beeping. She must have heard the sound on her way out because she saw fit to yell back in my direction between bouts of returning fire toward her much-older chauffeur.

"Hit 'one' and 'approve,'" she said, as sweetly as could be expected for a young woman in the midst of a shouting match that she had entertained many times before and would many more times to come.

It was clear that a pump required approval so that a customer could begin fueling, but it wasn't clear to me which one. The parking lot was empty, and there were no cars at any of the sixteen pumps in front of the building. When I looked out back, I saw that someone was at one of the pumps that I thought reserved for diesel vehicles. The car in question was a banged-up late-eighties Ford of some indeterminate model, and I knew that American sedans did not run on diesel during those years. Unfortunately, I had already successfully approved the pump and the driver had begun filling his tank by the time I came to that realization. It was at that point that Crystal walked back into the store. I had no idea how to stop the pump myself, so I made her aware of what I had done. I was half an hour into my first shift, and I had to wonder if I might have already gotten myself fired.

"So, I approved that pump, but I don't think you're suppos—"

"Oh, shit!" Crystal cried, muscling her wiry frame in front of me at the register and looking mortified as she hit a series of buttons resulting in the driver of the Escort Tempo Taurus giving her the international gesture for 'what-the-fuck.'

"Oh, man, I'm sorry. I didn't even think," I said, trailing off as I realized that I did not have a satisfactory ending planned for the sentence. Crystal stared at me; her lips pursed as she held her breath.

"Fuck, I can't do this," she said, bursting into laughter.

"What?"

"The first two pumps out back are gas. You're fine," said Crystal, approving the pump again and giving the driver an exaggerated thumbs up.

I felt my blood pressure spike again, like it had when I got picked on back at the Kirby interview. I had never been able to laugh at myself, and I always had a hard time not taking pranks personally. My fragile sense of self-worth didn't really allow for mistakes or being the butt of any joke that I wasn't in on. I knew that I was blushing out of embarrassment, and I decided to swallow my anger and turn it inward the same way I had learned in my youth. I knew how important it was to make a good impression and I didn't feel I was off to a very good start. I needed to do everything I could to conceal my true nature if I didn't want my coworkers to choose sides between picking me apart or handling me with kid gloves. It must have been a sorry attempt at stoicism because I think that Crystal picked up on what was going on inside of my head. She was doing a count of the bills in my till when she stopped, made eye contact with me, and spoke.

"None of this shit really matters, you know what I'm sayin'?"

***

After Donna walked me through that first shift change, Paul dropped into the store for what I understood would be a nightly visit. He had been out on the town, and he had brought a much older woman back home with him. The two of them were getting along very well, and they seemed to have some sort of previously established relationship, as far as I could tell. They also could have just been drunk, but more likely, it was some combination of the two. Whatever the case, Paul helped himself to a fountain soda and invited his lady friend to do the same. Donna finished her first cigarette of the night in time to instruct me not to charge Paul anything, even though she had earlier told me that employees only received free beverages while on the clock. The doublespeak didn't surprise me in the least, as my previous employment experiences had taught me that we were often trained to do one thing and then expected to do something else in practice. The fact that my manager was involved as a secondary party introduced a level of difficulty to the decision of how to proceed, so I decided to stick to the safest play in the book.

"Alright, two thirty-two-ounce fountain pops. It's going to be two dollars and twelve cents," I said, pausing while I located the appropriately labeled button on the register's keypad.

Paul looked at me for a few seconds longer than necessary. I glanced at Donna and then back to Paul, only to find that he was still staring at me.

He finally laughed.

"I'm just fucking with you," he said, producing a five-dollar bill from his wallet. Between Crystal's initial hazing and this little exercise, I saw a pattern. It wasn't clear whether they were singling me out or it was merely business as usual, but I definitely was not comfortable with it. I entered the payment, made the change, and shut the register, unsure if I had passed or failed, but glad the test was over either way.

I expected Donna to ask me why I had charged Paul for the drinks, but she said nothing of the sort. She produced her cell phone from her pocket and was very much engrossed in a spirited bout of T9 texting with one of the luminaries that surely graced her contact list. I glanced out at the pumps and throughout the store, unsure what the next step in my training might be but anxious to get on with it. It was clear that my trainer was in no such hurry, and so I stood there in the silence, waiting for my next instructions. It was uncomfortable. The idea of being on the clock and not being in motion or trying to help a customer made me nervous, so I picked up a dusting cloth and set my sights on the rack of chewing tobacco. I had started to unload the tins out of the dispenser and work the yellow cloth through the slots when I saw that Paul had re-entered the store and was on his way toward the register. I greeted him in the cheerful and robotic way that I had already learned to address all of our customers.

I thought that he must have forgotten to buy something, but he surprised me and came around the corner to approach the till. I watched as he grabbed a carton of Marlboro Lights in a box and a carton of Basic Menthol Lights 100's in a soft pack and rang them up. I saw him hit a few keys and was then a bit confused to see him pay with a twenty-dollar bill. Even considering the carton-price discount on both items, the total should have been a bit less than ninety dollars. I had the sense that something was off, but I opted not to ask for an explanation. My rationalization was that Paul must have been giving himself an advance against his paycheck and he would be settling up later in the week. It seemed like the most plausible thing at the time and Donna didn't act alarmed, so I opted to move along with my night. There was quite a bit to learn, and my trainer's lack of professionalism meant not much of it would actually be taught. For the most part, I was going to have to make it up as I went along.

Chapter Five

I have spent a good part of my life trying to break things down into smaller and more manageable parts. I realize that everyone does this, but I had a need to do it from a young age. As an eight-year-old, I typed out vacation itineraries for my family in hopes of bringing some sort of structure to what was likely to be a chaotic week that would otherwise result in quite a few of my violent tantrums. This is not to say that my efforts to bring order to the world have been successful, or to imply that they have led me to developing the ability to contain my frustrations in the slightest. I have had such trouble translating simple instructions into action that I have often frozen in place when not permitted to work from a script. I recognized these struggles as a child and sought out ways around the obstacles by employing a strict policy of honesty, following the rules, being prompt and generally attempting to eliminate as many potential variables as possible. In doing so, I noticed that those in authority started giving me the benefit of the doubt more often than not. If I wasn't able to act like a normal human being, I figured that the most convenient thing would be for me to limit my world to the framework in which I could feel most comfortable.

***

My training period lasted for five shifts, but I absorbed most of what I learned about working at the store during the first four hours of employment. That wasn't because Donna had a highly effective training style or because there wasn't anything more to learn, but likely due to the fact that she was thoroughly checked out.

She knew the tricks of the trade very well, but when we were alone, she could hardly be bothered to get up out of the old task chair in the back room. When I had questions, she would only be able to provide one half of an answer because she was perpetually three-quarters asleep. I would try to make sense of the vague hints she gave me about the way that certain things should be done, then clarify what I could with the other cashiers during the shift changeover. It hardly made sense for Donna to stay at the store after the second night, as she made no bones about her unwillingness to add value at any point. I felt complicit in enabling her poor behavior by the end of our week together, and I didn't like the way that made me feel.

When the store would empty out and I would ask Donna for the next task, she would respond as if she were the one doing that needed to be doing the guessing. She didn't seem to have any order of operations in mind, but I thought better of voicing my own opinions on how things should be done. Whenever her sleep apnea would let up, I would ask her things like which cleaners to use in the bathrooms and how many coffee filters to prepare for the morning shift. It always seemed like I was annoying her. I didn't know if she thought she could train me through telepathy, but it became clear to me that she didn't think many of the tasks needed explaining. As time went by, I figured out that it wasn't that she had an innate understanding of things—it was more that she understood that it didn't matter how the job was done. She was walking the line between a white-trash woman entirely in her element and someone who thought that her station in life was far beneath her for some unidentifiable reason.

When she wasn't sleeping or looking at me like I was an idiot, she seemed to be awfully preoccupied with making sure that she didn't miss a single opportunity for a smoke break. If there was anything to which she paid any attention, it was the clock that hung above the sink.

Even so, my first week moved along at a brisk pace. Each shift followed the pattern set forth on the first night—the training somehow becoming more and more hands-off as the week went on. Crystal's old man would arrive and honk the horn enough to be mistaken for a car alarm and Donna would show up late and in no hurry to work. She actually asked me to start without her on the third night. Luckily, Crystal was there to guide me through the finer points while we waited for my trainer's arrival. By the end of the week, Donna was only just clocking in after I had already gotten Crystal off of the register. It didn't matter one way or the other. It was clear that most of the employees were permitted to do whatever they wanted as long as they didn't do it in front of district-level management, and Donna took full advantage of that leniency. The only employees that didn't seem to go out of their way to break the rules were Crystal, me, and the woman that was working when I had come in for my perfunctory interview.

The cashier in question was named Rose, and she ended up relieving me after each of my first five shifts. Within two minutes of being formally introduced to Rose, I learned that she was a sixty-nine-year-old retired schoolteacher from Arkansas City, Kansas who happened to be on her third marriage. She arrived around an hour and a half early for her six-thirty shift each morning, and for some reason, she opted to drink coffee and read the paper in the back room rather than do the same thing in the comfort of her home. She was equal parts sweet old lady and angry old broad, and her pride in walking that tightrope was evident by the end of my first week. She struck me as the sort of woman who had secretly enjoyed having a long, hard life, and her singular complaint—and primary point of pride—appeared to be that she still had to work to afford her husband's endless list of prescription medications. While that may have been her only grievance, she definitely made a point to talk about it during the time that would have been set aside for discussing other day-to-day aggravations. The rationality of her obsessing over and bragging about her considerable burden didn't make it any easier to hear.

At the end of my first shift, Donna performed the changeover with Rose. Whereas she had explained what we needed to do at the start of the night, she offered no such information for the end. I gave her the benefit of the doubt, as the morning rush meant that the store was much busier than it had been, and she was apparently ready to clock out and go home. I stood on the platform and tried to find the correct balance between staying out of the way and learning how to do my job as well as I could. There didn't seem to be a method to Donna's madness, and she displayed no concern over her lack of efficiency, even though the shift was rapidly coming to a close and she was getting cranky. It seemed like the most logical thing to do would be to perform the tasks involved in the initial shift change in reverse order, but Donna seemed pretty set on just trying to do whatever she had time for between customers. As it was my first shift, I had no way of knowing whether things were going according to schedule. I only knew that there seemed to be a lot of room for improvement and no attempt to make it happen.

After about twenty minutes of trying not to shrug my shoulders at customers that I was not able to help, I was happy to see that Donna and Rose finally completed their shift change.

I watched as Donna scrolled through a menu on the clunky old register and began printing some sort of long report before jetting out the door for yet another cigarette break. When Rose made it through her first line of customers, she asked me to watch her own register so she could join Donna. I gave her the go ahead, but I had barely finished asking her if I should ring up customers or flag her down when she turned right around and headed back toward the till. With the way she was already coughing, I figured that it was for the best.

"Oh, child, you don't want to go out there."

"I don't smoke, so..." I said.

Rose paused and took a deep breath before shivering in disgust before she spoke again.

"That's good. It's a nasty habit, and I need to quit again."

"I don't think you even lit up, and you came back in looking white as a ghost, so I think that might be a good idea, too."

Rose didn't respond, instead opting to stare out at the latest surge of cars jockeying for pump position.

"I only smoke half the cigarette now. Just enough for a taste," she said, without making eye contact.

"Doesn't that get expensive, though?"

"Child, everything is expensive."

When I tried to make sense of Rose's logic, it made my brain hurt. It wasn't so much that I couldn't believe that she was stupid enough to keep chasing her fix; it was more that she somehow felt that she had enough money to do so that blew my mind. I didn't understand how anyone could maintain the habit, much less someone who had come out of retirement so she could try to afford marginally effective medication for a dying loved one. It wasn't only her, though. In the coming weeks, I would begin to see many of our regular customers come into the store for two packs of cigarettes a day, almost never opting to buy them discounted by the carton. The general argument was that to do so would result in more smoking, and as I learned, most of our customers were in the prolonged first stage of a long-term plan to quit. I reckoned that if I smoked two packs of Newports per day, I would have been spending a quarter of my pre-tax income on cigarettes every week. If I was willing to choke on the USA Gold Menthols, I could get it down to about half of that sum. If I opted for cartons of that brand, I would only be looking at spending about ten percent of my earnings on a disgusting, stupid, and harmful addiction. I suppose I could have considered such a fee to be a tithe to the god of death.

Chapter Six

For as long as I can remember, I have hated the idea of smoking and drinking. Some may be tempted to think this was due to successful indoctrination by the powers that be, but that was not the case. As I got older and started to think critically, it became clear that those who control the money have a vested interest in encouraging the public to engage in a wide range of costly and mind-numbing vices. My first shifts at the gas station confirmed this for me, and I began to wonder just how much higher the Philip Morris representatives might be able to get away with raising the price of a pack of cigarettes before people would say that enough was enough. Based on what I observed of my coworkers and the customers, I had no reason to believe that there would ever be any objection backed up by real action. It was disgusting to me. It's not that there is anything inherently wrong with a cigarette or a bottle of beer. There isn't even anything wrong with the corporations that profit from them; after all, the R.J. Reynolds Tobacco Company provides steady employment to millions of people around the world. The companies are blameless, as far as I'm concerned. The part of the equation that does deserve disdain, though, is the customer that continues to make the purchase. At some point, you need to blame the victim.

***

Donna returned to the store looking like she had been through a battle. She instructed me to record my ending numbers and headed off to the bathroom to freshen up. If Rose sounded like she needed to quit smoking, then Donna looked like she needed to go to the hospital. As Rose walked me through signing off on each other's numbers, I noticed that Donna was running the bathroom sink for an excessively long time. She hadn't spent enough time back there to warrant the sort of in-depth maintenance work that seemed to be taking place. I wondered whether she was trying to wake up or if she may have been taking her sweet time getting back to work. After about five minutes of the sink stopping and starting and watching Rose try and fail to maintain a good poker face, I decided to say something.

"If she's trying to cover up her smoking, shaving her head and burning her clothes would be the best place to start," I said.

"I know it, child. I never did get used to the smell. I think she has more than that to cover up if you know what I mean," said Rose.

As much as I could tell that she wanted me to take the bait, I decided to let Rose's words go without following up. It wasn't that I didn't wonder what she meant so much as it was that I never understood how I had anything to gain by participating in office gossip. My own guesses would likely be more entertaining than the truth, so any questions that I might have would only have led to disappointment at the answers. I had always liked the idea of maintaining the appearance of having a sort of moral superiority when it came to talking shit. Added to that was the satisfaction of knowing that I had cut Rose's chance to let me in on a secret off at the knees. I enjoyed creating these sorts of little awkward moments with others. I had no interest in being drawn into anyone's inner circle, so I would opt out of their little games and go play my own. If I would always be just as socially inept as I was in middle school, the very least I could do would be to try to convince myself that it was on my own terms.

By the end of my training, I was still very green, but I had exposure to the most common situations we'd deal with at the store. From then on, it would be more about repetition and refinement. Where others might have been settling into what they saw as an easy job punctuated with some occasional stress, I was already trying to figure out how to be the most productive gas station attendant that I could be. I tried to take in a bit of wisdom from every cashier and to see what they all agreed upon, but I found that most of the things that passed for common knowledge were poorly thought-out workarounds that didn't add any sort of efficiency or even adequately accommodate the user's laziness. Crystal and Rose were the only two employees that seemed interested in working hard or working smart, and Paul didn't seem to care one way or the other. Rose took the job seriously, but the passage of time had turned her into a statue. As for Crystal, she didn't seem invested, but she did demonstrate that she understood the fact that her life would get much worse if she didn't hold on to her position.

When Donna took her customary leave before the completion of shift change on my final night of training, Crystal saw fit to take the opportunity to fill in some of the lingering blanks for me. She volunteered some information and answered a few questions about work, but she was much more interested in sharing some of the same knowledge that I had denied Rose the opportunity to pass on.

"So, Donna takes a lot of cigarette breaks, right?"

"Well, yeah. She does seem to go out there quite a bit," I said, neglecting to mention that Crystal seemed to take her own fair share.

Satisfied that I had had my fun, I decided that I would let Crystal continue without attempting to shift the topic of conversation.

"You know, she ain't just smokin' squares out there."

I had never before heard the word 'square' in that context. I was able to deduce what it meant from the usage, but it didn't make any sense to me then and it doesn't make any more sense today.

"Oh yeah?"

"Nah. I mean, I don't care what you do at home—just don't bring that shit into work, right?"

"Don't we have cops stopping by all the time? It's pretty obvious she's doing something when she goes out there. She comes back in looking like crap."

"Like she goes out there looking better, right?"

"Oh man... your words, not mine."

"For real, though. She's doing some nasty shit out there," said Crystal.

"Whatever gets you through the shift."

"Whatever gets your bills paid is more like it."

"Okay, that's really not smart. Isn't there something about not getting high on your own supply or something like that, too?"

"Oh my god, haha," Crystal said, genuinely laughing.

"Hey, I've heard 'the rap music,'" I said, in a manner both defensive and played for comic effect.

"No, no, not that," she said, still laughing.

"Alright, then I have no idea what's going on."

"She's a lot lizard."

"A what?"

"You know, whatever gets her bills paid. A lot lizard," said Crystal.

"I... uh... Oh... *Ohhh*," I said, finally realizing what she was trying to tell me.

There was a pause.

"So that's dope," she said, as nonchalantly as possible.

Crystal went to the back room and gathered her hooded sweatshirt and the orange-stained Tupperware container that had contained her lunch. She was obviously getting anxious to head outside so she could smoke and start her drive back home.

"Okay, anything else that I should definitely know, going forward?"

"Yeah... Those things in the till you pull the bills out of when you get robbed?"

"The money clip alarm things?"

"Yeah, those."

"What about them?"

"They don't work for shit."

INCONVENIENCE

Chapter Seven

I don't know exactly how I acquired my work ethic, but it was probably passed down from my parents. It is not like they ever talked to me about the importance of hard work, but they modeled the behavior exceptionally well while I was growing up. I think that I inherited some parts of their individual temperaments which came together in such a way that it virtually assured that I would be a hard worker. It took me some time to grow into it, but by the time I was eighteen years old, I understood that the one thing that I could always control was my effort. I was conscientious to a fault, and when my hard work didn't pay off, I never thought about the possibility that my focus might be better placed on working smart. I would push harder and harder and attempt to burn and be seen burning more and more lean tissue. It was an inefficient way to get things done, but it was the only way that felt right to me. It was the only way that I felt that I could continue to maintain the moral high ground. It was the basis for the judgment that I'd silently pass down on my coworkers and the customers from high atop my pedestal behind the register. There was no better excuse for not risking anything or chasing my dreams than having ground myself into dust doing nothing but all of the things that everyone else understood that they were too good to be doing.

***

After spending my days off selling plasma to the local vampires and using the Internet to learn way too much about way too little, I was ready to head back to work and get settled into a routine.

I tried two different sleep schedules and found that I responded better to winding down a bit after work and sleeping with a plan to wake up shortly after noon. Following a few hours of wakefulness into the earliest part of the evening, I would take another nap before getting up to begin my day sometime around 9:30 PM. I managed to maintain that schedule through my off days for quite some time, aided by the fact that I didn't have any sort of social life of which to speak. As my friends had moved away from Mount Pleasant after graduation, my lifestyle wasn't likely to change at any time in the foreseeable future. I thrived then, as much as I do now, on the mundane and the predictable; I couldn't see any reason that such a schedule wouldn't work for me in the long term. It has proven to be useful for me to establish patterns, refine them, and stick to the script as much as possible. It doesn't matter what that routine might be. As long as I don't have to think and I only have to do it, the results are as close to perfect as they're ever going to be.

After my training, I developed a set of standard operating procedures designed to ensure that I could honestly say that I was doing my job to the best of my ability. These guidelines were always under review, but they were subject to change only after there was significant evidence that a paradigm shift was necessary. The basic idea behind the system was that all tasks should be done at the appropriate time and for the proper reason. I challenged myself to see how much work I could get done during each shift, and the volume of customers coming through the door had no effect on my expectations in that regard. If a customer were in the store, I would be straightening up behind the counter, and as such, I would often go through several microfiber dust cloths during a single shift. If the store was empty, it was my invitation to take care of tasks farther away from the register. I'd first stick to tasks on the outer walls before working my way from the bathrooms to the cooler doors to the platform behind the till. If the parking lot was empty, then I'd bolt to the recycling shed for some rushed bottle sorting and attempted cardboard baling. If there had ever come a time when I had completed everything, then I presume that I would have started over from the beginning. I never got that far.

When I developed my system, I decided that if someone had to be inconvenienced, the first preference in that regard would be me. This may seem self-explanatory due to the customer service environment, but I also made an active habit of putting my coworkers first whenever possible. Immediately upon clocking in, I would forego filling out the top line of my daily paperwork to shave anywhere between thirty seconds to a minute from the time spent getting second shift off the till. During times when I worked with others—in most cases, busy weekend evenings—I would start the shift by asking my cohorts what their preferred tasks might be for that particular night. If they didn't seem like they could be bothered to do much of anything, I was happy to let them stand at the register and collect money while I power-walked through the store and attempted to complete all of the duties. I made sure to stop at least once an hour to see if the other cashier might need to smoke or take a bathroom break or get something to eat, as I wanted to make sure that they didn't succumb to consumption from boredom. I made a point to first take on the tasks that each coworker had actively expressed a distaste for doing, but after some time it became clear that they would all eventually say the same things, albeit in a different order.

During my time working in restaurants, I had learned the importance of hustling. I took it so seriously that I would sometimes get dirty looks when I was seen working at a pace with which my coworkers were not comfortable. Some of my better friends ended up laughing in my face as I scrambled to make good use of all of the possible cleaning time before the next sink full of dishes would arrive. I was a true believer in the idea that if I had time to lean, then I definitely had time to clean. It didn't seem to me that others realized or cared about how much time they were wasting, and they didn't seem to understand the importance of task management. Looking back on it now, I think that they just had different priorities. They may not have cared about wasting time, money, supplies, or product, but they were acutely aware of the meaninglessness of all that wasted effort. I never got a grasp on that, myself.

When I came in to work the third night of my second week, I finally met another cashier. On that evening, I was greeted by a trust-fund hippie who I was sure had introduced himself as Morton. When I entered the station, he was listening to some sort of jam band whose music I couldn't identify and whose name I wanted to make a point not to learn. He seemed to be in an excellent mood, and he was perfectly nice, but people's niceness had never been enough for me to give them a second chance when they were goofy white guys who wore their hair in dirty dreadlocks and doused themselves in patchouli. Mr. Morton was flipping through an issue of *GQ Magazine* at the counter when I came in, which struck me as an interesting contradiction given that he was wearing a Rasta hoodie over his uniform polo. If I wanted to give him the benefit of the doubt, I could have written off the empty coffee pots and poorly stocked deli area as symptomatic of a rush of customers that I had just missed. I could have done the same when observing that he had not yet done his end-of-shift cigarette count. He erased any chance of either concession when he opened his mouth.

"Holy shit, dude, it's already that time?"

"Yep. Nine fifty-five."

"Oh, shit, cool. It's been really slow. So ready to get out of here, man."

"Alright. I'll try to get you out as soon as I can."

"Oh, dude, take your time. I'm not in a hurry. I'm Morgan."

I came to understand that it was going to be in Morgan's best interest to introduce himself in that way for the rest of his life. If nothing else, it could be said that Morgan was most definitely not in a hurry. I found that my initial instincts about the man were correct. He was, in fact, a trust-fund kid and he wasn't just listening to any jam band—he was listening to *the* jam band: Phish. He was serious enough about the band that he was going to spend the upcoming summer in the same way that he spent the previous two—following them around the country and volunteering in the chillout tent. As far as I could tell, he seemed to be living in the Americanized version of Pulp's "Common People." He wasn't majoring in any of the tried and true liberal arts programs, such as women's studies or sociology or comparative religion, and as it turned out, you could say he was actually studying when I came into the store. Morgan was majoring in fashion merchandising and design. He was unintentionally funny enough that I may have been able to forgive and forget the Phish and the patchouli, but I would never be able to do the same with the fashion. At the very least, I have always demanded that my fake hippies walk the walk. If someone is going to present themselves as something close to a caricature, I feel that they should commit.

Chapter Eight

While I was always very well behaved in school, I went through a couple periods of poor performance. The first rough patch began at my entrance to elementary school and ended when I was prescribed Ritalin a couple of months into the fourth grade. The change in my ability to focus happened almost overnight, and it was reflected in my report card. However, the medication came with some downsides, as I'm told that I lost quite a bit of what made me—*me*—during that time. I remember it as a shift from an interest in creative endeavors to more of an obsession with learning facts. I drifted away from *Dungeons & Dragons* and toward baseball statistics, and still haven't been interested in finding my way back. I gained an alarming amount of weight and left the methylphenidate-dependent part of my life one year later with a much better idea of what it felt like to pay attention. I maintained my grades until I hit puberty, but with the introduction of all of those hormones into my bloodstream, I found myself far more able to pay attention to girls than anything else. Unfortunately, the girls were more interested in paying attention to everything else, and so I lived and died with every word they said. If a school day ended on a sour note, I'd take it home with me and ruminate for hours on end, and my grades suffered as a result. I wasn't able to get out of that hole until I finally surrendered complete control over to the inner cynic.

***

Despite my distaste for everything that Morgan represented, he ended up serving a fundamental purpose in my development at the store. Performing shift change with Morgan presented me with a golden opportunity to learn through teaching. While he had been there for around four months when I started, Morgan seemed to have even less of an idea of how to do the job than I did. He was lazy, but his biggest problem was that he didn't really have a working memory of which to speak. He asked so many questions about the end-of-shift paperwork and the correct way to ring up items that I couldn't help but wonder how he managed when working alone. As a result, the few hours that we worked together each week actually went a long way toward convincing me that I knew what I was doing. It occurs to me now that he would have believed anything that I said, but his absent-mindedness gave me a chance to round out my training in a way that I wouldn't have been able to without his presence. If I didn't hate him for the shallow reasons that I did, I would have thanked him for his help—not that he would have remembered it.

I approached every shift as a puzzle for which there was no optimal solution. It was up to the worker to assign meaning for this pointless activity, and its relevance as a metaphor for life was not lost on me. This puzzle was always a struggle, but it was a struggle that needed to be undertaken in such a way that there would be some cessation of suffering—if not during my shift then hopefully during that of my relief. I saw a lot of responsibility attached to the job—not in making sure that the customers had a good experience but in making sure that the store ran as well as possible. I decided to begin my workday with the assumption that the previous shift had been a disaster and the next shift would likely be the same, and so it followed that it was my duty to transform chaos into something resembling order. I established the guiding principle that if there was something that I absolutely did not want to do, then that was the first thing that should be done. When I finished that task, I would reassess the situation and set out to defeat the next horror staring me in the face. I couldn't do it in my daily life, but at work, I faced all of my challenges head-on.

When I started my shifts, I would first focus my cleaning efforts on anything that the customer was most likely to notice. A secondary consideration that would often move tasks up the list was my understanding of what the last shift was least likely to have attempted to complete. In general, the more effort that a task might require, the more likely it was to need my attention near the beginning of the shift. An additional factor to consider when setting out to begin my routine was the presence and proximity of customers to the register. If a single customer was in the store, I would first try to take care of stocking cups and lids and brewing a new pot of coffee. If at least two customers were in the store, then I would focus on things like cleaning the counter and straightening out the impulse-buy items. As soon as the store was empty, I would leave my post to begin those pressing issues farther away from the till. Since customer-experience tasks took precedence, the order of operations would most often point me toward the restrooms.

Although the station was located just off the freeway, Logic Oil had made a point to presumptuously advertise on billboards both north and south of the store that the Pickard Street Shell had "Clean Restrooms." We were expected to perform hourly checks for routine upkeep and to give the bathrooms a full cleaning once per shift, whether they needed it or not. Management provided us with a power washer, but I found it too cumbersome to haul around; thus, I only ever tried to make use of it once. Shortly after I started, it became apparent that most of the other cashiers did not bother to make an effort to check—much less, clean—the bathrooms until the unlikely event that they were expressly told to do so. The policy was to accept customer complaints and thank them for bringing problems to our attention, but it wasn't as if any of the other cashiers were even interested in making a show of any effort to remedy a bad situation. Out of some bizarre sense of common decency, I did everything in my power to make sure that customers could actually grow to trust the signs at the side of the highway. I knew that my efforts were in vain, but that knowledge had never stopped me before.

As a rule, convenience store bathrooms are never a pretty sight. In most cases, the combination of running a skeleton crew of disinterested minimum-wage workers and the insane volume of customers seen every day ends up rendering pointless all attempts to maintain the premises. While Pickard Shell was not located at a major truck stop or just off one of the state's busier stretches of highway, the proximity to the local Indian casino and industrial parks ensured that our toilets always saw plenty of use. In general, most people are aware of what they are getting into when they opt to use a gas station restroom, and they usually will not think to raise the issue unless there is an obvious public health hazard. The truth is that a public toilet sees more use in one day than a home unit might see in one month, and it's no wonder that things get messy and often fall into disrepair. I saw these obstacles and the resulting lowered expectations as an easy opportunity to prove my worth. I thrived on situations where effort could substitute for skill and, therefore, appreciated the hidden value of the incompetence of my coworkers in every job I'd ever had. I found humor in the gross nature of the work, and the combination of the poor work ethic of my teammates and the even worse hygienic practices of the customers guaranteed that I'd never run out of things to laugh at.

At the first opportunity following shift change, I would hustle to the back room to grab the tools of the trade. While there were several different industrial strength cleaners that we used to clean the bathrooms, I was a firm believer that elbow grease was the most critical resource needed for the job. I didn't bother with rubber gloves, because they reduced the efficiency with which I could switch back to my duties at the register. I decided to trust the harsh chemicals to keep me and the customers safe from the myriad bacteria and viruses that I came across during every shift. I had to listen for the door chime so that I'd be ready to head back out to the deli sink to make a show of a scrub that most often lasted less than half the amount of time that it took me to get through the alphabet. I liked the idea that exposing myself to large amounts of filth was likely to result in my immune system being stronger than that of the average person, and my half-hearted attempts at washing my hands were my way of forcing that brand of pseudoscience on the unsuspecting public. I rarely heard the bathroom sinks running after the toilets flushed, anyway.

Once I got back down the hallway after the annoyance of collecting cash and putting it into the register, I was able to get on with what proved to be the most life-affirming part of my job. The first order of business would be to squirt the ammonia-based cleaner onto the ceramic surfaces of the urinal and toilets. I'd first do this in the ladies' room to give the caustic solvent time to cover as much of the surface as possible before I could return for the scrubbing of the basin. I would then spray the glass cleaner at the top of the mirrors, starting with the men's room, giving it enough time to drip down while I ran back to the ladies' room to begin spritzing the bleach-based surface cleaner onto the sinks and non-ceramic surfaces. With all the corrosive agents applied to their proper places, I would scrub the fixtures in the exact reverse order. It was an involved process, but I felt that it made enough sense to establish it a best practice. I liked the idea of identifying and developing a complicated routine to perform a simple task and then building out a rationalization until I was able to convince myself that the job couldn't be done any other way. In a bit of malicious compliance through working to rule, I also tried to see how many paper towels I could justify the store needing to buy every week. If that meant getting the job done well in the process, then that was an added bonus.

Chapter Nine

There was a time that I felt that if I wouldn't be able to become a good writer or a competent musician, I might have a chance of making a decent boyfriend. It seemed like a noble and attainable goal, and I didn't understand why other young men seemed to have such a hard time committing to such an objective. My early infatuations all followed a predictable pattern: a girl would treat me like a human being and I would fall head-over-heels-banana-peels in love with her. I'd make myself available to her at all times and start doing the sort of nice things that I would never do for someone in which I had no romantic interest. I'd listen to these young women tell me about all of the bad things that their boyfriends did and file them away as things that I would never do in a relationship, never stopping to think about the fact that I'd only ever hear one side of the story. I would see the same girls stick with these young men who apparently treated them like trash, never stopping to wonder why they would replace them with more extreme versions of the same boy within days of a soul-crushing breakup. I would ask my mother for advice, and she would assure me that the best path was to be a friend first and that the right girl would fall for me after she got to know me. As such, I would unknowingly manipulate these young women into a friendship with the intention of something more, only to find myself thinking more about their happiness than my own in the end.

***

The differences between shift changes with Morgan and those with Crystal were quite apparent early on. While it never seemed there was anywhere that Morgan had to be or had any idea how to go about getting there, Crystal straddled a line between being in a hurry and being dependent on rides that were always either too early or too late. Morgan's friends would often show up during shift change, and my efforts to get him out the door would end up being all for naught. He didn't let the fact that he was still on the clock dictate how much attention he was going to pay to his friends. On days that his friends didn't show up, he seemed content to spend just as much time attempting to pick my brain while I ran around the store. He was living at his own pace on someone else's dime, and there was never any evidence that he had or would ever have a care in the world. As for Crystal, it seemed like the only things she had more of than obligations were commitments, and the only thing she had less of than independence was freedom. When it came down to it, the only thing the two of them had in common was the only thing that mattered at the end of the night: *cigarettes.*

Whether it was Don's Restaurant or the McDonalds or the university's dining hall, my coworkers never stopped talking about smoking. They may have had other things to discuss, but most of the conversations revolved around things like the price of their brands, the merits of different types of lighters, and the timing of the next break. The cliquishness of social scenes had annoyed me all the way back to middle school, and I wish I could say that it surprised me to see the same mentality continue into the adult world. It seemed to foster a false sense of fraternity for which the only qualification was a common fault, and I didn't like the idea of anyone participating in an acquaintanceship that wasn't based on some kind of observed virtue. There wasn't any shared admiration, as far as I could tell. I had no interest in being a member of such a group, and I decided that anyone who did was guilty until proven innocent. As a result, I stopped making new friends sometime during my sophomore year of high school. Of course, I was always willing to make grand exceptions for any attractive women who invited me outside to watch them smoke.

When the old man was nowhere to be found at shift change, Crystal would pass the time with a display of chain smoking that belonged on the Olympic stage. Smoking three cigarettes within thirty minutes of clocking out wasn't out of the ordinary for her. In the early days, she would invite me to come out and keep her company and I'd decline because I was still focused on establishing my system. She would stand in the open doorway and adjust the volume of her voice so I could still hear her while I ran from the back room to the bathrooms to the register, regardless of whether or not I indicated that I was following along with her stream-of-consciousness ramblings. I enjoyed listening to her more and more every day, and I decided that the best way to make sure that neither of us ended up fired was to do the outside trash whenever she began pounding the coffin nails. With the occasional customer interruption factored in, more often than not, she would be on that third cigarette by the time that I finished with the trash.

There were eight different bins to empty, and I made a point to empty them all during every shift. I would head outside with eight empty trash bags, and regardless of the amount of trash in each bin, I would make sure to replace the bag in each one with an empty bag. In the early days, this meant that I would go through our back stock of industrial trashcan liners far in advance of the supply delivery day. As a result, I started emptying the lighter bags into the fuller ones and placing the remaining bags in the bottom of the bins so that the next cashier would theoretically be able to use them should they accidentally find themselves taking care of the garbage during their shift. I would usually end up seeing those empty bags exactly where I had left them, regardless of whether I had been granted a day off between shifts. As far as I could tell, Crystal was the only other cashier that ever bothered to take care of the trash, but she made no bones about the fact that she didn't feel it was necessary to go even an inch beyond the call of duty. I respected that she had both a work ethic and some healthy boundaries because I knew that there was no way that I'd ever be able to have both.

Crystal eventually took to following me around the parking lot. If she needed more input, she would ask a long series of rapid-fire rhetorical questions throughout the entire process. I'd give her brutally honest answers and watch her react with bewildered amusement as I consolidated the stinking bags and deposited them into the overflowing dumpster. When the old man took longer to pick her up, I'd include the other outside duties of filling the washer solvent and paper towels in the early-shift routine. I'd occasionally have to run back into the store to help a customer, and I would return bearing two more gallons of solvent or four more packages of paper towels. I would fill the dispensers every night and revel in the futility of the endless task, always challenging myself to go through more resources as if to prove some unidentifiable point to no one in particular. I'd thought Crystal seemed to be impressed at my persistence, but I may have been projecting my own thoughts onto her. I had made a habit of putting myself and my actions on a pedestal and then knocking that platform over in plain sight, hoping for a reaction. Most women didn't seem interested in validating the maladaptive behaviors I held so dear, but Crystal seemed to be different. Then again, they all did at one point, didn't they?

I never was able to get a handle on whether or not Crystal and the old man were actually married. She would cycle between calling him her boyfriend or her fiancé or her husband or her old man, with no discernable pattern. My best guess, given the evidence at hand, was that they were basically pretending to be married. That is not to say that they were running some sort of long con, but I believe that Crystal was the type of girl that considered herself married regardless of whether her man or the state had signed off on it. I don't think that women from her background were ever expected to be anything other than a wife and mother, and the pressure to make sure those things happened was probably such that the occasional little white lie was justified in the end. It didn't make much of a difference to me, as even if she'd been single, that wouldn't have meant that she was any more likely to see me as a romantic partner. She made her type pretty clear through her interactions with the customers. Suffice it to say, I didn't have the bad tattoos or bony torso, or lack of basic manners required to pique her interest. I think that she saw me as a harmless eunuch, which was the standard treatment I had gotten for as long as I could remember. I think that was the reason that she was so willing to let her guard down with me.

As I got older, I required less and less time to recognize when I'd reached the point of no return with the various objects of my affection. Whereas it'd taken a year and a half to get it through my head in middle school, by the time I met Crystal, I understood that I was a non-entity from the beginning. It wouldn't matter if I lost any sort of points with her because it was already clear that they didn't matter anyway. Getting into the grind of working nights and dealing with the worst that the general public had to offer had started to wear on me quite a bit. I found myself trying to hide how much of an asshole I was with each passing night, but it was impossible not to act like myself for at least some portion of my eight-hour shift. The most effective coping mechanism I had was the continued development of a patented mixture of dry wordplay and overt cynicism. When you factor in Crystal's growing level of comfort in our interactions, it's no surprise that I eventually treated her like every other human being. The only difference between her and the rest of the world was that I actually cared about her.

"Shit, I can't believe that asshole is late again, dude," said Crystal, lighting up her first post-shift cigarette.

"I can. It's not like he's been on time even once since I started," I responded, matter-of-factly.

"Hey, sometimes he's here like an hour before he has to be if he gets off early."

"That's not the same thing as being on time, is it?"

"Whatever, dude," said Crystal, laughing.

"Well, if he's here early when he gets off early, I guess he's probably getting off late tonight, right?" I said, deciding to poke the bear a bit.

"Yeah... no... motherfucker don't have a job anymore."

"Oh, he got fired, then?" I asked, knowing full well what was coming next.

"No, he fucking quit."

"You don't say?"

"They didn't pay him until his third week, and when they did, it was only for half his hours, can you believe that shit?"

"Well, that's gonna happen when you work under the table," I said, as if I didn't remember that he was working at one of the more reputable machine shops in the area.

"No, this was a real legit job. He was supposed to get a check every other week."

"Oh, he started in the middle of the pay period then."

"The what now?"

"The middle of the pay period. When you start a job in the middle of a biweekly pay period, your first check is only going to be for one week, and so you don't get your first full check until you're like three and a half weeks in," I said.

"Motherfucker, are you serious?"

"Yeah, it sucks, and it's a giant pain in the ass," I said, remembering when I had learned that lesson during the summer after my junior year of high school.

"Why didn't that fucker know that, though? How come he's forty, and you're whatever, and he don't know that shit?"

"I never said he didn't know it," I replied.

"Dude, shut the fuck up. He's a lazy ass but not like that. He never stops talking about cash."

"Well, hey. He's got a young family to support so I'm sure he wouldn't have quit without something lined up," I said, smirking.

"Fuckin' how are we supposed to feed both of us and then the fucking kids like this? This is crazy, man," she said, lighting another cigarette.

"Plural?" I said.

"What?"

"Kids. You didn't mention that you had more than one."

"Oh, I don't. His boys are living with us now."

"Oh, man. Yeah, how *are* you supposed to feed the kids?"

"Motherfucker."

"I think you summoned him," I said, pointing to the man of the hour as he rolled into the parking lot in the Earnhardt-mobile.

"Alright. I gotta get some scratch-offs before I go."

"Seems like a great idea," I said, thinking they were for the old man.

"Whatever. Don't judge me. You gotta play if you wanna win, right?"

It took me a long time to understand that when people played the lottery, they weren't looking to get rich. They were rarely even trying to make back the money they had spent. In ninety percent of cases, they would immediately put their winnings back into scratch-offs, and you could count on them to do that until they ran out of tickets to scratch. In some cases, they would take it to the next level and keep going until they had no more money to spend. I would venture to say that most people that played the lottery regularly were not so much addicted as they were dependent on it to take their mind off of their daily lives. Buying the tickets was only one of many ways available to do that, and it could be argued that it was one of the more harmless. That being said, some of the same people who would blow through hundreds of dollars of scratch-offs also had a taste for the little paper roses in the little glass tubes and the overpriced butane torch lighters. A full spectrum of ways for people to distract themselves was available, and many of the customers were interested in checking all the boxes at once. I never did get around to asking Crystal whether she was more of a fan of the S.O.S. pads or the Chore Boy.

Chapter Ten

As much as I have always tried to appease authority, it has gotten harder and harder for me to find a way to respect people in positions of power over the years. For all intents and purposes, I have endeavored to follow the rules. When I haven't followed the rules, it has rarely been due to lack of effort; it has usually been due to a lack of ability. The teacher who asked me to paste neatly in kindergarten was left with no other choice but to comment, "Tries," in the appropriate section on my report card. When my father would tell me how to do something, I'd find myself unable to put his verbal instructions in the correct order so that I could follow them as a step-by-step process. The pattern continued all the way through my childhood, and then I eventually had to deal with the realization that people in power were not infallible. When I started driving, my self-confidence was shaken by police officers who always seemed to find a reason to pull me over. It took me a couple of years to finally figure out that I wasn't always weaving from lane to lane and I wasn't failing to keep a consistent speed and my license plate wasn't dirty. I was terrible driver, but there was something else at play.

***

After a certain point, it became impossible for me to pretend that Paul was not stealing from the store. At first, I had thought that things were likely taken care of during paperwork or when he got paid, but there wasn't enough evidence to support that theory. When he wasn't using imaginary coupons to discount the price of cartons of cigarettes, he was taking money from our registers for supply runs and handing us receipts but never giving back the change.

He was quite comfortable taking items off of the shelf for his personal use without paying for them. I wasn't particularly bothered by any of this, as I was given no reason to believe that I would receive any blowback and his theft wasn't affecting my paycheck in any concrete way. Both Donna and Rose seemed to take a firm stance against what was going on. Given what I knew about Donna, I was inclined to take her concerns as more along the lines of false indignation than allegiance to any sort of moral compass. As for Rose, I'd thought she was terribly naive for a woman that had lived such a hard life until I realized that the propensity to assume noble intent had directly led to her struggles.

My indifference came to a full stop one morning about nine months into my tenure, when Paul arrived early and told me that he needed to talk to me after my shift. It had been busy for a weeknight, but Donna managed to get me off of the register in a respectable amount of time considering her standard late start. During the changeover, I was thinking about what Paul might have to say, and I couldn't think of anything other than the possibility that he may have done the paperwork to have me hired in. I finished up my own shift work, satisfied that I had come within a dime of zeroing out after factoring in the old hundred that I had to drop into the safe with my checks when the bill reader failed to cooperate. With my safe drops totaling $1420.00 and my report telling me that we'd brought in right around $5,000, it was a wonder that I had gotten much of anything done around the store. I stuffed my papers and stack of receipts into a bank bag, stuck it in the designated cubby hole, and stepped into the office. When I walked in, Paul held up a finger, finished counting a stack of twenties, and then told me to close the door. I felt my heart sink; not because I had done anything wrong, but because I couldn't think of any positive reason that the door would need to be closed.

"So, I called you in here to talk a little bit about your cash control."

"Alright."

"It sucks."

"Yeah?"

"Yeah. Your safe drops are coming up twenty dollars short here, fifty dollars there. Anything going on that I should know about?"

"Well, my paperwork hasn't shown anything being off."

"Envelope safe drops. Bills the reader won't take. Miscounted safe numbers. They're short. It happens, but it can't anymore, or I'll have to write you up. I've been sticking up for you with corporate, but I can't do that forever. So, uh... fix it."

"Alright, I'll do what I can, Paul."

"Thanks, Jim Sims. You can go."

The fact that Paul was stealing was the store's worst kept secret, but a lot of things made sense after our discussion. I had heard rumors of other cashiers having lousy cash control and getting the same talk, but no one ever seemed to get written up or fired. In fact, every cashier managed to improve their performance shortly after getting the talk, after which point another employee would develop the same issues with balancing their drawer. From the time I started, I had heard Donna gush about how Paul was a great manager and how he always had the cashier's back. It was easy to put it all together. Paul was stealing money, blaming it on a cashier, talking to them about the "issue," and moving on to the next cashier. The near constant turnover meant that he would never run out of employees to put through his system, and corporate had shown no signs that they would ever have any suspicions about what was taking place.

Paul's actions certainly didn't engender trust or respect from me, but what really shocked me was the continued lack of oversight from the corporate office. It was strange to me that the people who had the most to lose were those who were paying the least attention. As important as my employment may have been to me, if the talk resulted in my termination, a reasonable person would be quick to point out that I wasn't losing much. As for Paul, rumor had it that he was only making eleven dollars an hour in his position. The corporate office was apparently not concerned with the fact that a good portion of their profits was walking out the door with their store manager every time he worked. I had seen enough of the invoices to understand what kind of money the station brought in, and needless to say, the constant scamming should have been hard to miss. I found it difficult to take the district manager and his assistant seriously because they were showing their incompetence every day that they let Paul continue to have the run of the store. He was taking them for a pretty good ride, and he didn't even have any idea what he was doing. I couldn't help but think that I could do it better.

Just as I had memorized my favorite baseball player's statistics and the relationships between them, at some point, I stopped seeing transactions for the simple arithmetic problems that they were. I began to see the items that we sold as pictographic representations for the numbers found on their price tags, and I saw the same combinations of these symbols so many times that I was able to do the same with the transaction totals. I was able to make change in the same way as well. If a customer handed me a picture of Andrew Jackson, the difference due back from a pack of cigarettes from the second row was a ten, four ones, three quarters, and one dime. If the same customer had also presented taxable items like the middle-sized coffee cup and a gallon of windshield washer solvent, they were due to receive in return a ten, a one, two quarters, a dime, a nickel, and four pennies. There was no addition or subtraction needed. The register served only to keep a running record—only important in so far as the items sold could be audited at the end of the month.

The fact of the matter was that my ability to work with numbers was never something I worked at. People assume that individuals with outlier skills are blessed with some sort of all-encompassing intellect, but that isn't usually the case. In fact, sometimes it's the furthest thing from the truth. The last math class that I passed in high school was basic algebra, and that only happened due to a gratuitous curve. My interest in sabermetrics helped to highlight my talent for mental math, but I can't remember a time when I actually had to work to improve in that area. Memorization of the written word came just as easily, and I think this did me a disservice in the long run. I never learned how to work for something; as a result, when I did reach roadblocks, I just changed course. It happened with friends, with my family, with girls, and in college, and there was no reason to think it wasn't going to continue to happen unless I started to take matters into my own hands. I couldn't think of an intelligent way of doing that and have yet to figure it out. I'm still as clueless as ever—the only difference is that I've limited the likelihood of failure through the process of elimination.

Chapter Eleven

arly in my working life, it occurred to me that there was no such thing as an easy job. Some jobs were easy to keep, while some demanded more than others, but I was never able to think of coasting through work as deserving of a check at the end of the week. I was hard on myself, and always trying to do things more efficiently than I had in the past. I would see myself as both better and worse than my coworkers; better because I cared more than they did and worse because they managed to stay employed and even get promoted without breaking a sweat. I equated the amount of grief and anger and resentment that each shift brought me with my worth as an employee and a human being. I would see the other cooks, dishwashers, cashiers, and stock boys merely mail in their efforts and still get by, and I'd imagine what I could accomplish if I was as capable as they appeared. The idea of striving for something more seemed preposterous because I had never once felt the least bit competent in any endeavor that didn't come naturally. The more effort I had to exert, the more proof I had that I wasn't good enough.

***

By early July 2002, I had been working at the store for over a year, and I had been doing six nights a week since I'd been hired as a full-time part-time employee during the previous winter. I was putting in fifty-one hours at a regular rate of $6.05 per hour, after receiving a raise when I hit my six-month anniversary. I brought home about $275.00 each week, which nearly covered my rent for the tin-can single-wide trailer that I had been freezing and frying in since the previous summer. It wasn't much money, but I was spending next to none of it and opting to save as much cash as possible to get ahead of whatever disaster might appear on the horizon. My life consisted of working, eating, wasting time on the internet, and attempting to get enough sleep to manage to delude myself into thinking that I would be able to pull off the third-shift lifestyle without any long-term ramifications to my health. I wasn't going anywhere, and I had eliminated so many chances to strive for something more that my life was basically meaningless. I was overworked and bored and feeling cheated by no one other than myself. I hadn't put in a single job application since I was hired through the temp agency and my occasional struggles as a menial gas station employee convinced me that I had no business trying to sell myself as qualified to be anything other than what I was.

In that first year, I saw no fewer than twenty-seven cashiers come and go. I would say that over three-quarters of them left of their own accord, while others no longer had reliable transportation and the remainder departed after ridiculous disagreements with Paul or Donna. We never had more than nine clerks on staff at the same time, and almost everyone employed at the station was working a forty-hour week. Outside of the school year, service industry work could be tough to come by in a town like Mount Pleasant, meaning that we were all fortunate to be getting full-time hours in part-time positions. The McDonald's next door employed more than thirty adults, most of whom had kids and some of whom were commuting more than sixty miles for less than thirty hours per week. For most entry-level jobs in the area, the number of hours and amount of responsibility were directly related to the staff churn.

The high turnover had been expected when I'd started, as the college's summer break meant that hours had been cut everywhere; but reports from outside confirmed that the jobs hadn't come back the same way they had after previous summers. The state economy had entered a recession. Besides Logic and Next Door Food Store, our main competitor, only one other employer in town offered any sort of dependable work—the Soaring Eagle.

The Soaring Eagle Casino and Resort was the most desirable employer in the county, and for good reason. With a variety of jobs available for unskilled workers and an excellent benefits package, working for the Soaring Eagle was the most realistic way for an ordinary citizen of Mount Pleasant to make a living. Their strict attendance policy led to almost constant turnover in nearly every position. Even so, the backlog of applications was so long that most people called in for interviews had long since taken another job or stopped looking by the time they were contacted. Our customers who were employed at the casino would talk about things like insurance and paid vacation one week, then attendance violations and performance write-ups the next before ultimately disappearing, never heard from again. We'd lose our promising newcomers to the casino's guarantee of ten dollars per hour and then welcome them back after they failed to adhere to the stringent rules and regulations that the Saginaw Chippewa Indian Tribe placed on their employees. At Logic Oil, we weren't about to let something like a pattern of no-call no shows and poor cash control stand in the way of trusting someone to operate a register for forty hours a week. After all, it was a family business, and the emphasis was more on the family than on the business.

One such new hire we'd previously lost to the Soaring Eagle was an eighteen-year-old kid, Josh Turner. Josh was trained to work the morning shift, so my first interactions with him were at the end of my own workdays. He was a local guy that had recently graduated from high school and was looking for a job to bridge the summer gap between his senior year and his first semester at Central Michigan University. My initial reaction to him was that he reminded me quite a bit of Morgan, who had managed to stick around for my entire first year at the station. While Morgan had been more of a hippie poseur, Josh seemed to be more of a rocker type, a dying breed. They both smoked weed and talked about video games, and my limited interaction with Josh meant that I didn't have much else to go on if I was going to put him in a box. By the end of the week, it was clear that mentally, there was more to him than Morgan, but he had also made it known that there were other places that he would rather spend his time. I had looked forward to the idea of working with another person who wasn't a lazy idiot, but the fact that Josh had a brain and options meant that he wasn't long for the station. He moved on to the Soaring Eagle by the end of his first week.

Throughout my second summer at the store, Josh would often stop in during the middle of the night. He would buy a fountain pop and smoke a cigarette, his visits usually lasting about fifteen minutes. He happened to catch me listening to Dinosaur Jr. one night, which had sparked up a conversation about alternative rock of the 1990s, and our acquaintanceship took off from there. I began to take the opportunity of Josh's visits to start the process of cleaning the floors. While I vacuumed the rugs and banged them against the pavement, I would do my best to pepper the conversation with my cynical observations about life as a cashier in the most humorous way that I could. We'd switch the topic from music to entry-level philosophy and then to sports before finally moving it along to

Josh's hilarious and depressing experiences from his time spent cleaning carpets at the casino. All the while, I'd challenge myself to sweep up larger and larger piles of dirt and see how many times I could justify changing the mop water. After a few weeks of this nightly routine, it was evident that Josh had become the closest thing to a friend that I had made since my earliest days of college.

Despite my attempts to impart the wisdom I had gained during the previous year, I was unable to stop Josh from putting in a second application at the store. I couldn't understand why he would decide to leave an objectively better position at the Soaring Eagle, but he explained that they had informed him that they would not be willing to work with him on his schedule when the school year started. I couldn't see myself turning down ten dollars an hour for anything, much less the opportunity to focus more on studies that I now knew would set me up for a lifetime of failure. I had grown up believing that a college degree and hard work would virtually guarantee an exorbitant yearly salary of twenty-five thousand dollars, so I couldn't blame him for deciding to move forward with his education—misguided as he was, given that he wasn't going into a medical or engineering field. Young people always insist on making their own mistakes, if for no other reason than the desire to be the author of their own personal tragedy. As he was already trained, Josh was hired back in and slated to work the second shift in place of Morgan, who seemed to have disappeared on a vision quest.

When I came into the store to relieve Josh on the night of his first solo shift, I was already in a terrible mood. The police had followed me for the entire eight-mile drive to the station, and as a result, my heart was pounding. The rural Michigan cops always had a way of making me nervous. They were not above drifting in and out of my blind spot while they ran my plate and waited to see whether they could force me into making a mistake. If all else failed, they would often settle for pulling me over for that dirty license plate or perhaps having an unintentionally loud muffler. They were never bothered by the cars that sped past our two-vehicle cross-county caravan. On this particular night, I spent most of my drive wondering why they hadn't just decided to pull me over with their latest ready-made excuse. When I finally made it to the parking lot, I was relieved to see the patrol car make a U-turn in the middle of the highway and head back in the other direction.

I hated the cops in those days. I still can't imagine a time when their presence on the road wouldn't turn my knuckles white. They haven't even pulled me over in ten years.

***

When I entered the station, I saw that Josh had a line of rednecks dressed to the nines all the way back to the cooler. Based on the night of the week and the inebriation of the customers, the store was undoubtedly looking at another case of the casino's summer concert series laying waste to everything in sight. To minimize the damage, I clocked in as soon as I could. As I walked toward the till, I was waved over to the coffee pots by a customer clad in leather pants and a pristine black T-shirt featuring wolves, flags, and the meticulously grizzled visage of one of the biggest names in pop-outlaw-country. Through a combination of monosyllabic grunts and crude body language, he told me that the coffee pots were empty and he was none too pleased about it. I went to work on remedying that situation as Josh continued to plow through the endless line of suburban cowboys and the women who tolerated them. I latched the nozzle underneath the metal frame and angled the coffee pot to drain the burnt remnants of the previous brew into the sink before heading to the register.

"So, you couldn't stay away from the allure of the store, I see," I said.

"Ha, there's nowhere else I'd rather be," Josh replied.

"It is pretty fantastic; I'm not going to deny it."

"No, seriously—they're just going to be a lot more flexible here. Something would suffer during the school year, and I kinda value my social life too much for that."

"That makes sense, then," I said—lying—as I imagined what it would be like if my social life were important enough to warrant such a change. "So, how's it going?"

"Fine, I guess. Crystal left at nine."

"How was she tonight?"

"Angry, haha."

"That makes sense, too."

After I finished counting in my drawer, I headed back to the fast food area and moved the empty coffee pot back to the burner. I loaded the grounds into the basket, pressed the button to begin brewing, and returned to the platform to continue with the shift change.

"So how have things been here?" said Josh.

"Busy. Fine, I guess. One thing about gas station work, you know—it's never interesting," I said, hoping that Josh would still pick up on my dry humor.

"Haha, I've heard just the opposite," said Josh, condescending enough to show that he knew where I was going.

"You know, when you tell someone you work at a convenience store, I think they assume it's basically *Clerks* or something like that, but they're wrong."

"Well, it's not black and white," said Josh.

"That's true, there are nuances. But also, Kevin Smith really glamorized what we do here in that movie. I don't feel like it has ever been even half that watchable. It certainly hasn't been anywhere near that tolerable."

"You're in it, though, so it's not going to seem that interesting. There's no hockey on top of the store, but for an outsider, it's definitely something different," said Josh.

"Don't come at me with your logic and your critical thinking. I'm trying to rattle off some witty insights here."

"Haha, I'm sorry... I'll refrain from shitting on your point."

It was at that point that another wave of customers interrupted our conversation, which was just as well. If I wanted to get Josh out at a reasonable time, I was going to need to focus a bit more. After verifying my drawer against Crystal's ending numbers and doing the same with Josh's final reading of the safe, I turned around and set off for the back room to count cigarette cartons. I had only stepped off the platform when a well-dressed, older black gentleman at the soda fountain managed to get my attention.

"You got a mess over there," he said calmly, gesturing with his hand in what seemed to be the direction of the bathrooms. I immediately began power walking down the hallway to survey the damage, only to hear the man's voice again. I spun around.

"Nah, man, over there," he said, this time pointing in the direction of the still-brewing coffee pot, which I realized was draining faster than it was filling. I had once again forgotten to unhook the handle when I removed it from the sink.

"It looks like you forgot something."

"Yep," I said, rushing past the man to turn the machine off and grab the basket so that I could empty it into the trash.

"Looks like it got the rug, too," he said, continuing to give play-by-play.

"Yep," I said, attempting to cut him off.

I can't stand it when someone points out my mistakes and continues to talk about them while I'm in the process of addressing them. Even to this day, it takes everything in me to control my temper, and I wasn't able to do that on this particular occasion. After emptying the hot coffee grounds into the trash and closing the nozzle on the coffee pot, I made my way to the predictably empty paper towel dispenser. I headed to the back room to retrieve the necessary reinforcements, and when I returned to the storefront, I found it nearly vacant. Without the customer standing in as a surrogate for my rage and thus helping me stay focused, I lost the plot. I picked up the aluminum coffee urn and tossed it hard enough into the stainless-steel sink to result in the sort of violent crash that I needed to hear to remind myself that something needed to change. It was all Josh could do to pretend that he didn't notice what was going on. After throwing the soaked rug outside in a much less satisfying attempt to make a point, I headed to the back room to fill the mop bucket in complete silence. As quickly as my anger had erupted, it had subsided and left me feeling nothing but embarrassment. I placed the wet-floor sign in front of the coffee machine and got to work.

With normalcy restored, I returned to the platform and set about continuing the shift change. I dropped to my knees and checked the safe using the stick and noted that most of the change was already used. I popped back up to my feet in hopes of learning that Josh had a lot of coins that he needed to sell me but was greeted by the sight of another rush of concertgoers. I moved on to cartons, single packs, and lottery tickets and then back around again to check my numbers against Josh's. He had written them down too early and thus would have to do some recounts and make some changes. He wasn't having a smooth shift, but he was dealing with it in such a rational and calm manner that I couldn't help but be impressed. I would have seen such a shift as a fight to the death against both myself and the unwashed masses, but Josh seemed resigned. It was a more measured apathy than that of Morgan, and an appropriate response to a screwed-up situation. I think he understood that such a night was not going to be the norm. I was thinking about offering him an awkward and ill-advised compliment when he saved me the embarrassment and spoke again.

"I actually meant that *Clerks* was filmed in black and white."

Chapter Twelve

We have much more control over when we reach a breaking point than we really care to admit. There's a certain romance to the idea that you can get pushed past some arbitrary level of bullshit after which you can't take it anymore, but that is more of an excuse for bad behavior than anything else. You'll often hear someone announce that they are about to blow a gasket, but I've found that people rarely end up exploding if there isn't anyone around to watch the fireworks. We're all much stronger than we realize, and people would be amazed by how much they could put up with if they just kept pushing forward. For me, the more that I have taken the path of most resistance, the more tolerance that I have been able to build up for dealing with it. Now, dealing with something has rarely meant making it more manageable; rather, it has often just meant shutting my mouth and taking a straight line right through the chaos. I've put my head down and proceeded as if it was business as usual through all manner of hopeless situations, but I haven't ever figured out how to actually fix anything. I've made things worse, and I've just patted myself on the back for not complaining about it.

***

Donna trained me to make fresh coffee every two hours, regardless of whether the store had sold any from the previous brew. To ensure there was never a time when the customer wouldn't have coffee available, I would rotate between the two regular pots. We didn't have two urns of decaf, so there were occasional short windows during which the unleaded stuff was unavailable had anyone ever tried to make the mistake of purchasing it. The stainless-steel pots were supposed to be rinsed between uses and cleaned every night by brewing a bag of Blue-Sky meth-soap crystals and letting the mixture sit for an hour. Occasionally, someone would ignore the sign placed on the spout and help themselves to a cup of industrial cleaning solvent. They would often berate me for their own lack of ability to read the sign, but it was par for the course. The very same people would also tell me that they liked our coffee because it was always fresh and then talk about the fact that our competitor's pots were visibly stained. I didn't know if they'd made the connection and I found it more interesting to leave that question unexplored. After all, the customer was always right.

I estimate that I drained at least five times as much coffee as I sold during my tenure at the gas station. It seemed as if I was always preparing a stack of filters so that they were ready to go, and every other day I would be the one to bring out more packets from the back room so that my coworkers would have the grounds ready to go during the morning rush. I found a certain kind of Zen in the idea of plowing through the task without giving thought to how much the guidelines were getting in the way of working smart. I found a lot of humor in the wastefulness of the whole process. It reminded me of my time working at McDonald's, where I never stopped putting the meat on the grill, transferring it to the warming drawer, and tossing it into the trash when it didn't sell within fifteen minutes. More than any sort of attempted convenience-store culture jam, I liked being able to focus on hard and fast guidelines regardless of whether they made sense. I learned to cherish my role in maintaining the absurd order of things, knowing full well that each time I pushed the rock up the hill, it would also be my responsibility to get it back up the other side when it invariably tumbled over the apex.

As much of a grind as work had become throughout my first two years, the addition of Josh to the roster made it that much more bearable. I was still enjoying most of my interactions with Crystal, and I knew that I had feelings for her, but I also recognized that they had more to do with proximity effect than anything else. That is not to say that I was able to shut them down, but I recognized that she had faults, and that was quite a step forward from where I had been in the past. As long as I wasn't actually talking to her, I was able to stop pedestalizing her and think of her as another flawed person in the midst of doubling down on her bad decisions. As for Josh, he represented more of what I wanted to be. He was younger than me, more intellectual, and involved in a relationship with an attractive, bright, and genuinely interesting girl. He seemed to be living what I had observed as the best-case scenario for myself as I entered college, and for once, I wasn't even particularly jealous. As far as I could tell, he was one of the few that deserved the good things that had come to him. I suppose that's why we hit it off so well. Beyond Crystal and Josh, my time at the store was defined by working hard enough to justify my fragile sense of self-worth and laughing hard enough to stop from drowning in self-doubt.

I would often joke with Josh about a vague concept that I liked to refer to as the "immaculate shift." Such a night of work was anything but perfect, but the moniker was not merely an attempt at irony. For a shift to receive such reverence, there were specific qualifications that it had to meet. It could not just be the result of constantly being slammed by customers, as no work could be expected to be done in that case. In an immaculate shift, there would need to be a perfect balance between theoretically having the time to get everything done and dealing with a level of customer traffic just high enough to render all efforts completely for naught. Calories would be burned, money would be collected, cleaning supplies would be used, cigarettes would fly out the door, and the self-correcting system would continue to lurch in place. The store would be left in the exact same sorry state as I had found it, as if I had set out to treat the station with the same respect that one is asked to treat a national park. These sorts of shifts were most often seen on Thursday nights during the school year, but during the summer, they tended to coincide with the casino's summer concert series. With the pattern established and identified, it was decided that Josh would be enlisted to help me out for the first five hours on those specified nights.

The longer I spent spinning my tires and failing to gain traction in my work and in my life, the more I began to play around with the idea that work ethic was more a scam invented by those in power than a moral virtue. It became impossible for me to ignore the distinct feeling that such a predictable compass was not meant to serve as a guide for the user but was actually installed as a means of control by those in middling positions of authority. There were endless platitudes to commit to memory, but the most important of all was the wholly empty idea that hard work was its own reward. I had heard variations on that statement for so long that it had stopped having any meaning, but during those long, immaculate evenings, I finally came to understand. If hard work was both the means and the end, then it would follow that the only motivation for busting your ass was not just the chance to, but the necessity of, continuing that into oblivion. I suppose that this thought was born out of Nietzschean gallows humor, but I believed it to be correct more and more every day. It was hard for me to even consider the idea that I was taking a subjective viewpoint on objective reality. I had learned the lesson through the most excellent teacher of all, and it wasn't something that I could ever forget.

I eventually decided that I would float this idea at Josh. I wasn't looking for confirmation that I was on the right track, but the validation that my worldview was entertaining and interesting to someone other than myself. On the few occasions where I had tried to talk about things that I found worth exploring with the other employees, I tended to receive blank stares and dismissive one-syllable responses. Josh and Crystal were the only coworkers with whom I'd felt comfortable sharing any of my crackpot theories, and so I would often bounce things off of them under the guise of carrying on a genuine conversation. Crystal seemed to be more entertained than interested, but Josh seemed to enjoy exploring the ideas with me. I liked being able to share the small amount of knowledge that I had gained about the world with someone who could appreciate the absurdity of it all. Truth be told, Josh already knew more than I did, but I don't think he understood that in the beginning. I could have said the same about myself as an eighteen-year-old—in fact, I am still trying to work back to the clarity of those years. There was something so pure about the singleness of mind that I had during that time. I used to know everything, but now I've learned too much.

"So, Josh, I was thinking the other day," I said, well aware that one thing I had never understood was the art of starting a casual conversation.

"Uh oh... anything worth sharing, James?"

"Well, I've been thinking about the concepts of work ethic and efficiency, especially as they would relate to working for a small company that might own a couple of dozen convenience stores in the Mid Michigan area."

"Seems pretty specific," Josh said, laughing.

"Well, you know—start small, right? So, here's what I was thinking... I currently make six ninety per hour. I'm paid that amount regardless of how hard I work, and that's understood. But what I'm curious about is how much I actually get paid for one unit of work. So let's say that there's a minimum amount of work that I have to do each hour to keep my job. We'll call that amount 'x.' Basically, you could look at the average amount of work that you do each hour and call that 'x,' but there are people here that do nothing and they still get to be employed, so 'x' is probably closer to whatever it is they do all day."

"Haha. Go on," said Josh.

"If you're supposed to give a hundred and ten percent effort, then you might produce one point one x worth of work every hour. Good for you. But you still only get paid what you get paid for an hour of work. If I put in one hundred and ten percent, but I am still just paid six ninety per hour, you could say that I've reduced my wage to like, six thirty per x. It's junk math and likely faulty logic, but I'm standing by it."

"No, I get it. But here's the first problem with your math," said Josh.

"There's a problem, is there?" I replied, in mock indignation.

"You work at least twice as hard as anyone else," said Josh.

It was absolutely true, and it absolutely was a problem, on many levels. Though I was aware that my efforts were wasted, I was so indoctrinated that I couldn't make use of that knowledge. While I was on the clock, I had a hard time thinking about the work I put in as being anything more than the amount needed to meet the minimum requirements of the job. If I was functioning as a cashier, then maintaining perfect cash control wasn't anything more than what I was supposed to do. That made perfect sense, but most of the things that management tasked me with doing didn't have such easily quantifiable results. How clean does a convenience store restroom have to be for you to say it is clean? Can you say that you have finished dusting shelves if your work leaves any remnants of the sort of filth that accumulates from second to second in any given environment? I knew the folly of my perfectionism, and I was able to control it in my day-to-day life, but I could not do it when I was on someone else's dollar. I had long since bought into the trap, and for some reason, I was proud of it. It was the only thing that I had over anybody else, and thus, the only thing that allowed me to tolerate myself.

After Josh left that night, I went about my business in the usual manner. I took care of my duties using the same method as I always had, and for once, it seemed like my efforts led to the desired results. It was a slow night, and there was more work to do than ever and no excuse for it not to get done, and I found myself enjoying the focus that the shift had afforded me. By the morning, I felt like it was one of the rare shifts that I could say that I had done my job well and not feel like I was grading myself on a curve where I would benefit from the lack of productivity of my coworkers. The store looked worlds better than it had when I had arrived, with the counters and floors well scrubbed and the shelves and fast food supplies stocked to the point that they wouldn't need attention until I returned later that evening. I was sweaty and exhausted and dirty and sore and I smelled like cigarettes, coffee, bleach, and ammonia and I wanted nothing more than to go home and take a shower and head to bed, happy that I had once again confirmed my status as the most obedient of the wage slaves. I had taken the cognitive dissonance of the night's earlier conversation and refused to let it pull me down into the predictable mire of piss-poor performance, and I was still patting myself on the back when I finally noticed that Donna was a half an hour late.

My conversation with Josh had served to fan the flames of discontent. I spent the bulk of the evening working very hard to stomp those flames out like a cigarette and had nearly succeeded. However, it was not to be. In fact, it was the same as it had always been. I had recognized the path that I was on and wrote myself a new manifesto, only to be put back in my place by the truth. This time, that truth came by way of the late arrival of a coworker, and that proved to be enough for me to once again feel the powerlessness inherent in my perceived lack of options. I knew the pattern. I would default into my self-appointed role as chief cynic, doling out attempts at dry and pessimistic humor and false wisdom to anyone whose presence I could stomach. I would pretend that being in on the punchline somehow made my life less of the throwaway street joke that it had become. I would laugh at my perceived mistakes before anyone else could possibly notice them and somehow expect that to result in others not holding me to basic standards of competency. It was all one giant, maladaptive coping mechanism, and I knew it. I'd like to say that I had an epiphany that resulted in my escape from convenience store hell and set my course for a better life, but I'm not in the business of telling lies quite that farfetched. The truth of the matter is that on the morning of June 17, 2003, in a carefully considered act of defiance against the tyranny of the self, I stole an ice cream sandwich.

SHIFT CHANGE

Chapter Thirteen

While I tried to tell myself that I needed to keep an open mind, spending more and more time around people hadn't done anything to deter me from further developing a rather misanthropic belief system. I grew up finding myself annoyed at other people for doing nothing other than existing, and I had a hard time understanding how anyone who was paying attention could feel any different. During college, insulation within my small group of friends had led me to soften my outlook, but the education that I received at the store changed all of that. I had tried to write off my old thoughts as the symptoms of adolescent moodiness, but I was amazed to see just how well I had understood things all the way back to the sixth grade. The concessions I had made for the behavior of my friends had served to convince me that I should be more of an accepting person, but that was undone during my early time behind the counter. Living the convenience store life meant that I only saw people at their worst, and my new level of isolation resulted in forgetting what merits I had seen in my friends in the first place. After a while, they started to seem more and more like regular people, and that wasn't going to be good enough for me. I was already quite a ways down the road to becoming a world-class asshole.

***

On the morning of the great ice cream sandwich heist, Donna woke me up with a phone call. There was a mandatory meeting at eleven o'clock, and as I had been attempting to sleep in the ninety-degree heat of the trailer, I had to find a way to take a full shower and put on clean clothes in under ten minutes. I managed to do that and then jumped in the car and headed off to my destination at a much faster clip than my usual paranoid observance of the speed limit dictated. I had just noticed that I was going to make pretty good time when I saw the long-expected police flashers in my rearview mirror. It was all I could do not to laugh as the officer strolled up to the car and began the process that would result in the receipt of a one-hundred-dollar speeding ticket, an increase of my monthly car insurance rate, and my late arrival at the store meeting. The cop gave me the go-ahead to continue on to my destination ten minutes later, and thankfully, my rage didn't boil over until she had returned to her own vehicle. I spent the rest of the trip unleashing an impressive stream of obscenities, to the point that I was hoarse and out of breath when I pulled into the lot. I rushed into the store, and I can't say that I was surprised to learn that Paul had called off the meeting. Before I headed back home, Donna made a point to inform me that I wouldn't have been held responsible for not showing up, either way.

When I came back for my shift that night, I was still simmering. I decided that the best way to deal with my anger would be to continue to try to control the things that I could control. While Paul had been the one to call the last-minute meeting, I was the one who put the pedal to the metal. I could get as angry as I wanted about what had happened, but my feelings about the situation and the citation had no bearing on the fact that I had to deal with the fallout. I got so focused on psyching myself up to rise above the issue that it actually seemed to be affecting the initial count of my till. No matter how many times I counted the tens and fives, I kept coming up with sixty dollars in Hamiltons and fifty-five in Lincolns.

It wasn't like that sort of discrepancy had never happened, as there had been times that a cashier would be hit with a transaction directly before the end of a shift and they would still have gone ahead with the changeover. However, in this instance, the bills were paperclipped as if they were the proper amounts. I glanced at the last shift's paperwork and found that Rose had indicated that she had left fifty dollars in both tens and fives.

When Rose had made similar mistakes in the past, I had always followed protocol and asked the other cashier on duty to verify the count. The errors were usually quite clear, as making the necessary changes to the paperwork would bring Rose closer to zeroing out for the shift. In other cases, the issue would only become evident when the daily paperwork was completed the next morning. Rose maintained exceptional cash control whether her paperwork showed it or not, so she would never hear about these sorts of minor transgressions. Paul was not likely to bring up such an issue to Rose even if her cash control was lacking. She was an old woman that shouldn't have been working in the first place, and more importantly, had been a witness to some of Paul's more nefarious activities. She was untouchable. I suppose that the combination of that knowledge and my own recent change in attitude was what led me to sign my initials next to her ending till numbers, pocket the extra cash, and move on to the next task like nothing had happened. It seemed like the most logical thing for me to do at the time. It made sense.

Working the third shift did not do me any favors when it came to viewing myself in a good light. In truth, most of the people that I came into contact with were in the store for questionable purposes. During the last hour of the shift, I could count on seeing some people on their way to work, but that was not the case for the bulk of the night. The sort of customers that came into the store on third shift were generally out looking for a fix of some kind, whether it be lottery tickets, tobacco products, junk food or the alcohol that we had thankfully not been grandfathered in to sell. My patrons had empty, lifeless eyes to go along with vacant, undead souls that they were trying to bring back to life with anything they could jam into their systems. I couldn't bring myself to feel empathy for them, and the most maddening thing was how I saw myself starting to fit right in with them. They were damaged and broken, and it was undeniable that I had a lot more in common with them than I did with anyone else. I just hadn't found my drug yet.

I never understood the appeal of getting to know random people before I worked at the store, and I appreciated it even less after. Some of my coworkers thought that the people were the best part of the job, but I was much fonder of the weekly paychecks. The other cashiers would often say that the customers ensured that it was never boring, but I felt the exact opposite. There were only six or seven different types of people that came into the station, and seventy-five percent of them fit into two of those categories. As a result, it was easy to predict the way that each interaction would go. It didn't take very long to memorize the most common transactions and the words exchanged in the process, but what really struck me was the incessant use of the same clichés and phrases from day to day, month to month, and year to year. From colder than a "witch's tit in a brass brassiere" or "a well-digger's ass in the middle of February," to "fair to middling" and "better than they deserved," it seemed that most people were working from the same script. I tried to take solace in the fact that if nothing else, the droning of the average customer was so redundant that it could sometimes be effectively tuned out.

Whenever I would stop at the store outside of my own working hours, I could count on one or more employees standing in the parking lot and puffing away on cigarettes. Often, those who were smoking outside the station weren't even on the schedule for that day. I couldn't imagine why someone would want to hang around their place of work while they were off the clock, regardless of the false friendships that they had decided to entertain during their short time employed there. If it weren't for the fact that my superiors were the worst offenders of all, I would have been much more amazed by the sheer number of breaks that people were permitted to take. If the day seemed to be dragging or hectic, or someone was having a personal crisis or enjoying an unusually pleasant day, or it was just rainy or happened to be really sunny, it was going to result in one of my coworkers inviting the others out back for a cigarette. Whatever the situation, a joint smoke break was always warranted. I would not be surprised to learn that we'd lost one full employee's shift worth of productivity every day to those adult children imitating poets, rock stars, and cowboys by taking the opportunity to try to kill themselves a little bit quicker. Truth be told, I usually wished that their efforts yielded faster results.

For all my abstinence from the various existential crutches, I didn't feel that I had any more of an idea of how to deal with life than the customers or my coworkers. They may have been in various stages of death and decay, but for the most part, they seemed happy, or at the very least, resigned. While they were reaching out for anything they could grab, I was making believe that I possessed imaginary virtues that would eventually pay off and ensure that I got what was coming to me. There was a basic script of inner dialogue running through my head—a never-ending series of self-congratulatory platitudes—and I was so very proud and so very bitter about the way that I martyred myself every day. I had the idea that I'd eventually be able to fake stoicism well enough that I'd finally be content with myself, and everything would fall into place. I knew that wasn't going to happen, but I was so in love with the idea of my imagined good triumphing over the world's supposed evil that I refused to back off. I found it very easy to rationalize the escalation of my immoral behaviors and laugh to myself about the dichotomy of man. I shrugged it all off, as if nothing that I did could ever be as bad as everything that everyone else did every second of every day.

It's not as if I hadn't known that I had vices, and it's certainly not as if there hadn't been a direct relationship between the stress incurred during my shift and how much I'd leaned on them to get me through the day. While others smoked and played lottery tickets and planned their evening's worth of alcoholic and herbal refreshments, I set my sights on the vast quantities of free junk food at my disposal. From the fountain pop to the expired hot dogs to the day-old donuts, there was no limit to the number of salty and sugary calories available for my consumption. I spent quite a few terrible nights trying to figure out how much trash I needed to eat before I was able to counteract my feelings of being a total failure. The dopamine rush associated with the escalation to the actual theft of merchandise and cash was much easier to incorporate into my strawman framework of self-respect. It wasn't as if I was ever going to stop trying to work myself into the ground and it wasn't as if I would ever be adequately compensated; so in a sense, I was proud that I had finally taken things into my own hands. I told myself that one man's reasons were another man's excuses, but I still had no interest in walking even a few steps in anyone else's shoes.

Chapter Fourteen

I never had to go out of my way to learn how to do the things that I know how to do. Along the same lines, I don't have many memories of getting objectively better at anything. Driving was one of the activities that I didn't take to very well, and I remember thinking that it seemed to demand far more skill and concentration than it would be worth. On the off chance that I would be able to figure out what I was doing behind the wheel, it wouldn't be as if having a license would open my world up into some sort of teenage paradise. I knew where I stood. I made a fool of myself every time I drove during driver's education, with a rotating cast of my peers sitting in the back and cracking easy jokes about my inability to master the simplest of tasks. I struggled so much that my instructor actually spoke with my parents and my school's guidance counselor in an attempt to discern if I might have a severe learning disability. I could not transform instruction into action, and results actually seemed to be inversely proportionate to my effort. In the end, I aced the written exam, and the teacher went on vacation before I needed to complete my final road test. However, that didn't stop him from endorsing my ability to pilot a two-ton death machine.

***

Shortly after I started taking advantage of Rose's mistakes, the condition of my car took a much anticipated and quite drastic turn for the worse. The vehicle in question was a 1989 burgundy Dodge Daytona with low mileage, and I had purchased it from an old woman with money borrowed from my parents. She'd said that it had belonged to her daughter and was now only taking up space, so she'd been willing to part with it for a thousand dollars. It was turbocharged at one point—not so you'd really notice it, of course—and it had a digital instrument panel; thus, it was the nicest car that I'd ever owned. I wasn't in love with it, but I was thrilled to be driving. Since I didn't really have anywhere I needed to go, and I never had any money during college, I had not owned a vehicle since the summer after I received my high school diploma. The campus of Central Michigan University was the only location in Isabella County that could be considered walkable, save for the small downtown business district of Mount Pleasant. The public transit system was all but non-existent, so a car was a necessity if I were ever to plan to move on to a more ambitious place of employment. I suppose it also offered the added bonus of the ability to take someone out for a date, but that was more of a theoretical benefit.

Based on my history with old beaters, I knew when my car was beginning to fall apart, and I knew that there wasn't going to be much that I could do about it when it happened. To a person working for minimum wage with nothing in the bank and bills on the way, the average trip to the auto mechanic for anything but the most routine maintenance may as well have cost a million dollars. The low-end estimate of one thousand dollars to replace a head gasket in an older vehicle isn't any more affordable, because the money is still just not there. In high school, I had leaned on my parents when I saw the telltale warning signs pointing toward the possible end of a car's functional lifespan, but I hadn't even started paying them back for this one, so I wasn't going to give myself that option this time around.

I was trying to force myself into growing up, and some part of me was hoping that the upcoming loss of transportation might scare me straight and suddenly give me the ability to fake the confidence and competence needed to start moving forward. I had a feeling that it wasn't going to work out that way, but at that point, I couldn't tell the difference between my negativity and making a rational assessment of the situation. Given how bad things were, there was quite a bit of overlap.

While I knew what was coming, there wasn't anything I could do to stop it, which didn't really make the situation any less stressful. With no acceptable options, all I could do was try to self-medicate through comedy. The next time Josh and I did shift change, I took the opportunity to share my non-thoughts, with the hope that if nothing else, I could get a little bit of codependent validation. As always, I got right to work on that the second I walked through the door.

"Have you noticed that every fuel supplement that we sell recommends that you add it to every tank of gas?"

"Haha... Good evening, Jim. Well, they're not going to tell you not to use their products, are they?"

"No, but I mean—Is anyone dropping twenty-five dollars of additives into each tank?"

"I doubt it, no—that's kind of ridiculous."

"Well, I think so, too, but—picture this: You buy a new car, and it's under warranty. It gets you from point A to point B, ninety-nine percent of the time. You're really happy with it, and then that one percent comes around, and you need to take it to the shop. What's to stop the car company from entering into a deal with STP that means they will not honor the warranty unless you're constantly buying all of the fuel treatments?"

"Nothing, I guess, but I don't think there's anything to worry about."

"There's just so much stuff like this, though."

"Well, it is a gas station, and we do sell stuff."

"Well yeah, but it's not just STP, though."

"What, you think Velvet Revolver is in on it, too?"

"Well, Scott Weiland, at the very least... Seriously, though. There are so many things that you're obviously supposed to do and so much stuff that you're just told you need to do that it's impossible to tell the difference. If you did everything you were supposed to do all the time, there's no way you could keep it up. There's no way you'd have the time or the money. It wouldn't be sustainable. And then you'd start cutting corners and something would fail on you, or something would just go wrong, and it would reinforce everything you'd been told, and you'd have no one to blame but yourself."

"So... today we're angry at... entropy?"

"Yeah, I know, it's unreasonable. But routine maintenance—Jesus Christ—car maintenance, house maintenance, lawn maintenance, dental maintenance, heart maintenance, lung maintenance, relationship maintenance, pet maintenance, spiritual maintenance. Let's not even get started on planned obsolescence. Fucking hell, it is all one big trap."

I stopped talking, as it was time to count in my till and I wanted to give Josh a chance to offer his input. After about a minute of silence, he spoke.

"I don't even bother with anything but gas-line antifreeze."

As it turned out, my instincts about the car ended up being on the money. That is to say, the Daytona sputtered to a coughing death less than two weeks later. When it finally happened, I wasn't surprised to be taken with the feeling that I had done everything but whatever simple upkeep was needed to keep the car on the road. I had plenty of time to think about that as I walked the final two miles to work that night. When I made it to the station, I did my best to turn my anger into more entertainment as I worked through shift change. As for Josh, I think he understood that I was in a bad situation because he volunteered to pick me up for work on the nights that he wasn't already stuck at the station himself. He didn't say how long he would be able to do it and I didn't intend to find out where his generosity ended at the last minute, so I spent most of my shift trying to figure out what else I would do. Not that many choices were available, but that didn't stop me from trying to conjure some up out of nowhere. After I was satisfied that I had rolled nothing around in my head for long enough, I admitted that the best solution would be to plan to walk to and from work and never count on getting a ride. It was better than any of the other nonexistent options at my disposal.

Chapter Fifteen

I have always felt that people needed to be shielded from their most self-destructive tendencies, myself included. It's not that I thought that I knew best, but I just didn't see enough evidence that people had the necessary instinct for self-preservation. It was one thing to treat others like they didn't matter, but when I'd see people treating themselves in the same way, the nihilism of it all was tough to take. My first thought was not to help them. My humanism was always giving way to hate; consequently, I wished good people mostly the best and bad people only the worst. I couldn't help judging them by what I saw as the inevitable outcomes of their behavior. I could see people's lives stretching out in the same way that I saw my own, like the future was becoming more of a foregone conclusion with every second. I felt a lot of sympathy for everyone but—with a few noteworthy exceptions—I felt even more contempt.

***

After years of listening to customers whine about the fact that we didn't have an ATM, the company eventually had one installed. I was sad that I wouldn't be able to see the looks of disappointment on the faces of our patrons as we tried to save them from their worst impulses, but all was not lost. Our automatic teller machine and the proximity of the casino came together to create some extraordinary opportunities for some downright depressing and equally entertaining stories. We began seeing customers come into the store and take cash advances from their credit cards, all while extolling the virtues of the low transaction fees associated with our "ATM *machine*." After inputting a "PIN *number*" and completing their withdrawal, they would leave the station for a few hours and inevitably return. The cycle would repeat until they would hit their daily limit and then move on to their other cards. When they had run through all the cards, they would become desperate. While some customers would attempt to sell us their watches and necklaces and rings for amounts entirely outside of the monthly costume jewelry budget of a cashier, others would approach the counter with a "really good feeling" about those scratch-off lottery tickets.

As it had been explained to me, most credit cards have a cash advance maximum well below the account holder's credit limit. We were the only store in town that would allow people to buy lottery tickets with plastic, and so we were able to "help" the down-on-their-luck by allowing them the chance at a small amount of cash with which they could head back to the casino and presumably win it all back. Customers would buy two hundred dollars of scratch-off tickets, only to hand them back to be run through the machine, sight unseen, and exchanged for what would usually amount to between twenty and forty dollars in winnings. We would occasionally see someone break even, but for the most part, that was not the case on my watch. I assumed that my experience was out of the ordinary because it seemed implausible that anyone would be so eager to exchange such a large amount of credit for such a small sum of cash. I couldn't imagine that a person would ever be stupid enough to do that and pay interest on top if it didn't eventually result in a large payout. As such, I didn't feel bad about setting aside the occasional unscanned winner for myself.

In the beginning, it astonished me to see how much of a value people placed on convenience. It is not that I didn't understand the merits of a quick and easy fix, but it seemed like our customers had a very low bar for what constituted inconvenience.

We sold some items at prices four times what they sold for at the Meijer down the street, and that store was considerably more expensive than the Walmart across town. A customer would talk about their time being worth the difference, but they seemed unaware that the money they were spending came as a result of selling a greater amount of their time to their place of employment. We took advantage of them at every opportunity. We sold gallons of prediluted engine coolant for twice the price of the concentrate. We sold twenty-ounce bottles of soda for twice the price of a two-liter. We nickel-and-dimed our patrons into oblivion; we did with a smile, and they didn't seem to care one way or the other. As a result, what sympathy I had for the customer dissipated into disgust, and that led me to become more daring in my interactions with them. If I wasn't going to make money, I was going to make sure that I had a good time at someone else's expense.

Cigarette prices continued to climb throughout my tenure at a rate much faster than the rate of inflation. While a few people switched to cheaper brands or began rolling their own, I don't remember a single person who'd said that they were quitting who hadn't come back in within the next few days for a restock. They would refuse to switch to buying cartons, citing the valid point that they would want to smoke more if they always had them so readily available. When a customer would tell me that they were spending two thousand dollars a year on smoking, I would grab a calculator and do the actual math for them. I'd ask them how much they were smoking and how often they bought lighters and show them the final amount, with the caveat that it was too hard to estimate future medical costs. The reactions would be the same each time—the customer would express exasperation at the results, and they would walk out with a fresh pack of smokes. I started to see it all as being just as well. The customers who came into our store and ignored their own better judgment deserved everything they got, up to and including early death. It was nothing personal, though.

I found that the customers were very slow to catch on when I gave them shit, but I would occasionally run across someone who would call me out. I'd counter with more honesty, owning up to the fact that I was envious of the money that people had and making it known that I felt terrible for people who didn't feel they could change what they admitted was as a bad habit. I found that cutting my matter-of-fact cynicism with some sappy oversharing usually disarmed people enough that I was never in hot water for very long. The best target for this type of interaction was someone with a little more going on in their head—that is, someone with more going for them than myself. The only person I talked to regularly who fit that description was Josh, and so he would often have the privilege of shrugging off a bit of my needling. We'd finish up a shift change, then I'd start with something inflammatory, and he would usually hold back his responses and always seemed to be giving me enough rope. I preferred to take the strategy of hanging myself before anyone else could take control of the noose. I think he was more entertained than concerned, and that's all I really ever wanted from anyone.

Just as I had done with my friends in the past, I held off from judging Josh by the same standards that I applied for the general population. The hypocrisy of this decision wasn't lost on me, but basically, the more I got out of my interactions with a person, the less likely I was to frame their personality as the sum of their faults. I'd see the things that I didn't like about them as integral parts of who they were and thus a portion of what drew them to me in the first place. It was arbitrary, but it made good sense to me when I was younger, and for the most part, it still does today. I had gotten away from giving anyone the benefit of the doubt in my early years at the store, when I would completely write people off without any chance for redemption. The passage of time and the ongoing incorporation of my shadow self had somewhat brought me back to the sort of clarity that I had enjoyed during my late teens. I'd like to say that it was all for the best but having a functional consciousness has always been a mixed bag for me. I think that I am happier as an automaton.

The topic of cigarettes was never far from my mind, and it served as a great jumping off point for some of my better conversations with Josh. He smoked throughout his entire time working at the station, and was aware of my thoughts on the habit, but I don't think he held them against me. Perhaps he did, but he may also have thought our interactions were worth listening to me on the soapbox. Whatever the case, had he been the sort of person who was going to take offense to my opinions, we wouldn't have gotten along as well as we did. I had a lot of things to say and I hadn't been around anyone who appeared to want to hear them for quite a while, so I often went overboard, and I think he dealt with it as well as one could expect. I liked the idea of trying to find a proper balance between the profound and the ignorant, but most of the time, I ended up having to settle for the profoundly ignorant. It was as worthwhile for me either way, so it didn't really matter. I was happy to have a receptive audience for my musings, and I loved to open my set with something guaranteed to get some sort of a reaction.

"People act like they don't understand why cigarette prices keep going up because they don't want to admit that they're powerless to stop acting like idiots."

"That's kinda harsh, haha."

"Well, I mean... what's the point of complaining about something that you can't change? Why not focus on your own agency? You can't change what we charge you for a pack of Reds, but you can change your behavior. As long as you are going to keep buying cigarettes, why would we stop raising the price? There's absolutely no point in a protest that isn't backed up with action. All that does is remind you that you aren't the sort of person who isn't willing to do anything but bitch. What's the point? I don't think anyone needs to go out of their way to remind themselves that they're a loser."

"Yet here we are, again, Jim."

"Haha, indeed, and believe me—I probably have a better argument for that than you, but that can wait for another day. So let's say that instead of the big price increases, we raise them by one cent per day. How many days do you think we could do that before you or anyone else stopped buying them? I bet it would go on for a lot more days than you'd think. You might see some smokers go to another store, but most people would keep stopping here out of habit. What's one more cent every day, right? Eight fifty a pack by this time next year and we could totally get away with it. That's all capitalism is. You could raise the price quickly to see what people won't pay and adjust it from there, or you can do it like this, basically imperceptibly over time. How many of these people have stories where they said that they'd never pay more than a dollar a pack?"

"I think you need some new material."

"Am I skipping again? Try the other side. There's a good one about crackheads that I don't think you've heard yet."

"Heh. The funny thing is that you need to smoke more than anyone I've ever met in my life," said Josh, counting out some change and placing it on the counter.

"Not just cigarettes, right?"

"I'm just saying," he said, eliciting a laugh from both of us.

"It's good material, though, right?" I asked, looking for some validation.

I handed Josh his pack of Winston Lights and slid his customary payment of exact change off of the counter and into my hand, took a demonstratively deep breath, and decided to get in one last thought before he headed home for the night.

"You know, as this job gets more and more involved and the economy gets worse and worse, they're going to start requiring degrees."

"Like a bachelor's in convenience?"

"Inconvenience is right, buddy—No, probably more like an associate's in customer service."

"I know a guy who got his Bachelor of Business Administration in Hospitality Management, and he works the front desk at a motel now."

"Working in his field, then. Seriously though, if we are going to keep moving toward a more service-based economy, service job employers will have to have a way to sort through applicants. It will be totally justified, too."

"Well, they have burger college."

"Wait until it's accredited," I said.

"Well, I guess you want the best people, so you're going to take people with demonstrated skills."

"That's exactly what I'm saying. It's going to happen."

"So, what about the people that can't cut it?"

"Well... Did you end up reading *Player Piano* yet?"

"Heh, no. I read the back, though. And that brings up another question—what happens long term, when service jobs are made redundant?"

Chapter Sixteen

A certain amount of willful blindness is a prerequisite for undertaking most endeavors in life. If you pay full attention to the facts, there is too much information to take in, and you must decide what is relevant. You need to select a suitable model to measure your success against because there will always be plenty of evidence available to suggest that you're actually failing. This makes excellent sense as a survival strategy, but unfortunately, it also lends itself to a tendency to discount things that don't fit your preferred narrative. It starts innocently enough; after all, it is reasonable to think that if you can't solve a problem, there is a good chance that there is no solution. However, that is not usually the case, and this is when you will see things get swept under the rug. It is why you will find gazes averted from the facts, and that is how small problems become nearly insurmountable obstacles. We all know these things, but it's incredible to see the lengths we will go to ensure that we don't have to deal with them. If you're always busy, you can productively procrastinate your way toward perfectly feigned innocence. If you do it right, you will never get called out for it.

***

No one was particularly surprised when Paul Jackson stopped showing up for work in the fall of 2004. At the time of his disappearance, he had only recently returned from burning up his vacation days, both company-awarded and self-prescribed, on the beaches of Miami.

While he was out, Donna acted as the store manager, and she wasted no time making it known that she had spoken with corporate about our absent leader's behavior. I'm told that Paul showed up four hours late on his first day back, sunburnt and still drunk and in no way ready to work. As the story goes, most of the other days weren't much better. With the revelation of his inability to keep his hands out of the till and the fact that his planned ten-day break had lasted sixteen, it disappointed me to see that the company had allowed him to return to the store in the first place. My only direct interaction with Paul during that week was on Wednesday morning, when he somehow showed up early. He seemed unusually awake and not the slightest bit repentant or worried, despite the rumors swirling around since his return. While I didn't ask, he informed me that he would be leaving, but the way he framed the circumstances suggested that it was of his own accord. Last I heard, he was running an office-cleaning business back down in Florida.

There was a brief moment when I thought that the company might decide to go all in on chaos and actually promote Donna, but that didn't end up happening. I suppose that was for the best, but it would have been quite an entertaining disaster. Instead, the corporate office slotted Pamela Spadafora, manager of the Coleman store, into the vacant role. My initial impressions of Pam were favorable, in that she seemed like a tough and smart lady who was there do her job and wasn't likely to put up with a lot of bullshit along the way. She was in her late forties and divorced and had lived hard and laughed often, and she had the lines to prove both. She was the sort of woman that Donna seemed to imagine herself to be, but as far as I could tell, there weren't many similarities between the two of them outside of their possession of the same number of arms and legs and their shared interests in cigarettes and alcohol. I'm sure that further research would also reveal that they both enjoyed food and television, but I was never curious enough to find out. I will say that I never heard any rumors about Pam selling blowjobs in the parking lot, so she probably did not share Donna's entrepreneurial spirit.

Seeing what Paul was able to get away with in his position led me to think more and more about what I could do to supplement my own income. The store's refusal to upgrade to UPC scanning meant that there was an awful lot of unearned trust placed in the cashier, and so my best bet was to exploit that system to its fullest potential. It became a game, as I tried to avoid direct theft in the most creative ways that I could imagine with my small brain. I would add items for myself to customer transactions, especially when the local construction crews would come in to secure the day's rations with the use of a company credit card. I'd do cash transactions in my head and hit non-active register buttons for show along the way, only to pocket the payment when the customer would leave. If someone bought an item that was buy-one-get-one-free, I would fail to notify them and refund the price of the free item to myself. If anything was noticed, I'd admit my "mistake" and provide a refund and a free fountain drink for the customer's trouble. I dreamed up and refined these processes every day, and it didn't take long before my repertoire included over a dozen of these low-rent scams.

As a night shift cashier, I watched the audit process dozens of times over the years, and I was always amazed by the speed at which it took place. It wasn't that our store was particularly large, but the woman who took inventory was in and out of the store very quickly, considering that she worked alone. I spent most of the time she was in the store going about my regular duties as if she wasn't there and thus paid very little attention to her methods, so I could only imagine that there was some sort of unseen magic taking place. I would entertain myself by listening for patterns in the sounds of the clacking of the ten-key device hanging at her side, and before I knew it, there would be yellow tags throughout the store showing that she had accounted for all of the products. We would see the results on the corkboard in the back room a few days later, with those departments showing shortages highlighted and those with overages ignored. Either way, we'd never receive any direct feedback. The process would repeat the following month—none of the individual ending numbers making the slightest bit of sense and even less so when viewed together.

I might have read the situation wrong, but I think that it was the lack of coherent results that led the auditor to enlist the services of an assistant. When she did, there didn't appear to be any evidence that the change a positive difference in the accuracy or efficiency of the process. If anything, the inventory started taking longer and longer, as a fair amount of time was spent reexplaining the basics to a rotating cast of characters overmatched by the demands of the position. The change had introduced another variable into the equation, and the fact that no one stuck around for more than two months meant that the results couldn't be tracked one way or another. One thing that was certain was that the company was spending more money to reach the same inconclusive results. Given the information at hand, I thought it would stand to reason that perhaps the company should have started looking at the commonalities between the failed attempts at taking care of the inventory process, but it was not to be. The comedy of errors continued throughout my entire tenure, but in the end, the auditor did eventually bring along one short-term assistant that ended up making quite a difference—at least as far as I was concerned.

During my time at the store, I came into contact with dozens of attractive women on a day to day basis. For the most part, they were garden variety, perhaps a bit older than they might have been if I had worked on the side of town closer to the university. I was never very interested in the sorority types or the women that would frequent the casino, and so neither tended to leave a lasting impression on me. I'd appreciate them while they were there and forget them minutes after they left the building. However, there were rare instances when the station was graced by the presence of a girl who had something a little different, and these were the times that made the job momentarily worthwhile. In the span of thirty seconds, I'd find myself smashed senseless by someone extraordinary, only to see them walk out the door and in all likelihood, never return. For the most part, I just did my best not to ruin the short time I had with them by saying something any more stupid than what was already required by the duties of my position.

If you've been following along, you're probably going to assume that the auditor's new assistant ended up as one of those girls. While that is true, my extended time spent around this particular young woman meant that I wouldn't wind up getting off anywhere near that easy. Thinking about it now, it's pretty clear to me that she was under eighteen years old and thus too young for me in the legal sense, but I hadn't even thought about that at the time. We never exchanged a single word but having her in the store made me feel almost exactly the way I had felt during those fleeting moments in high school when it seemed like something great might happen. I was drawn to her, but when thinking about what I could ever have done about that, I was as clueless then as I would have been if we'd been the same age. She even seemed like the type of girl that I would have liked in those days, in that she managed to pull off a perfect balance of complete focus on the task at hand and genuine apathy for everything other than whatever was going on inside of her own head. As it stands, knowing that she existed was a particularly exquisite form of torture that I was happy to have had the chance to suffer.

If there was anything that was going to make me pay attention to something other than the filth and disrepair that the store was falling further into every second, it would be a cute girl. In fact, I'd found my eyes opened to dozens of things that just happened to have needed to be done while standing directly in front of the till on that night. From counting cash to dusting the windowsill behind the lottery tickets to rotating the chew by expiration date, it seemed there'd been an endless list of tasks that could only have been completed with the assistant in plain sight. I was busy trying to commit the girl's existence to memory in the least conspicuous manner possible when the auditor approached the counter, disrupting my line of sight. She began counting the candy bars in the milk crates stacked in front of the platform, and it was then that I happened to glance down and finally realize that for all intents and purposes, she was just mailing it in. There was no way that she could have accurately counted all of the ninety-nine-cent packs of chocolate Skittles in such a short time, especially given the haphazard way that we dumped the boxes into the bins. She was spitballing and ballparking her figures—rendering the entire exercise pointless.

It wasn't until I understood the sloppiness of the work that went into the monthly inventory that I began feeling comfortable stealing products off of the shelves on the regular. I started keeping track of the approximate value of the merchandise that I took throughout the month, and no matter what I did, it didn't seem to make too much of a difference when it came to the audit. The lack of attention paid to the reports together with the faulty methodology meant that the numbers didn't say anything. I'd make off with close to two hundred dollars in prepared sandwiches one month, only to discover that we'd finished the month actually showing in the black on taxable food items. The next month I would move on to a different department, and there would never be a correction even though I was no longer walking out with three-quarters of our stock of turkey grinders. Between subsidizing my monthly grocery bill and continuing to siphon off a few dollars from the till here and there, I found a way to make a tenable situation that much more sustainable. In essence, I put myself on a pretty lucrative welfare program. The only remaining question to be answered was how much of a handout I deserved to receive.

Chapter Seventeen

People do not like to take responsibility for the consequences of their actions, especially when they do not result in a positive outcome. In fact, some people are so averse to the idea of being held accountable that they will refuse to take credit for the things that they do right so they can claim they have no culpability when things go wrong. The wide receiver is quick to give all glory to God, no matter how much work he put in to make sure that he was ready to make the catch. When he fails, he can take solace in the idea of the divine plan. He may even wonder if his failure came about as karmic payback for a past transgression. I don't know if people really believe the stories they tell themselves, but I do think that they manage to stave off some of their existential dread by congregating with others who share the same superstitions. Life is a heavy burden; the idea that you might be to blame for your failures is a lot to take, and it is comforting to find a way to pretend that isn't the case. If you do something terrible, there will always be someone there who will allow you to repent, and your sins can be washed away. There is fire and brimstone, but there is also a chance for redemption, and that's a whole lot less frightening than the reality that it's all up to you. Even if you play your cards right, it might not be enough. It's no wonder that people try to find something to convince themselves they can believe in.

***

Through the use of her own proprietary blend of bullshit, Donna managed to persuade Pam that it was in the store's best interest if she had weekends off. She remained in her position as the assistant manager, but her absence on Saturdays and Sundays meant that she would no longer have the responsibility to take care of the books. Since Crystal was only able to work on Sunday mornings, it was under these circumstances that I found myself promoted to shift supervisor and switched to a hybrid schedule that was sure to wreak further havoc on my circadian rhythm. Donna saw fit to rush my training on the company's buggy and archaic accounting system over the period of two predictably unfocused days, and afterward, I had an even better sense of how Paul was able to do what he had done. The fact that the company had not caught on to what had been taking place until it had been directly pointed out to them suggested a level of disinterest that was tough for me fathom, and I saw no evidence that anything had changed since his departure. I found myself wondering about the possibilities. After all, it wasn't as if my promotion meant that I would be in a position to stop taking advantage of the situation as I saw fit. The raises I'd received during my time at the store along with my overnight hazard pay meant that my new title did not actually come with a raise.

For better or worse, the switch to working mornings on the weekend made my continued employment at the store that much more bearable. While I had to deal with more customers during second shift, I was able to spend more time with Crystal. Aside from filling in the gaps in training on books, it was interesting to get some time with her outside of those moments during shift change. While we didn't spend a great deal of the time in conversation, we did gain a better sense of each other. I think she came to understand where I was coming from a bit more, and she probably got a kick out of her increased direct exposure to the way that I entertained myself while dealing with customers.

With every weekend morning we spent together, I was relieved to find that she was less and less of a special person. I was able to talk myself out of the small crush I had developed on her. When she took the opportunity to tell me that she was pregnant, I finally began to see her as more of a flawed human being than anything else.

Due to my affinity for working with numbers, it didn't take very long for me to build up a high level of confidence in my abilities in the office. I started testing how quickly I could finish the daily paperwork, so that I could take full advantage of having another cashier on hand to work the register. I found myself integrating the bookkeeping process into my standard order of operations whenever possible—the old computer's slow processor provided ample opportunity to make that happen. It wasn't out of the question for me to hit the enter key on the keyboard, run to the restroom to apply Sunny Streakless, return to the office to submit three more lines of data, and then head back to finish cleaning the mirrors. I particularly enjoyed carrying out absurd behavior patterns that could be justified as the most efficient path toward getting the work done. Just as I had always said I would, I made a point to be visible doing all of the little things I had done before my promotion. In this new phase of my career, the primary witness for this Sunday morning hamster wheel business was Rose.

I stopped covering up Rose's mental slip-ups shortly after the company hired Pam, and instead decided to make sure that they received as much attention as possible. I didn't have anything against her, but I recognized a relatively simple way that I could use the old lady's failing faculties for my own means. By making sure that Pam was aware that Rose was no longer as sharp as a cashier should be, I knew that I would be able to establish plausible deniability for more substantial future attempts at keeping my finances in the black. I began taking random bills out of Rose's safe drops, resulting in her cash deposits not matching her paperwork. She was always annoyed and apologetic, and I don't think she ever suspected anything. She'd ask me to pick up breakfast for the both of us at the Bob Evans next door every Sunday, and she would always offer to pay. I would insist that she eat first, only to help myself to a few dollars from her till while she enjoyed her scrambled eggs and toast in the back room. I stuffed my face between transactions, and when Rose finished smoking her post-meal cigarette, I would resume taking care of the store's most labor-intensive tasks. I think she really appreciated everything I did for her.

I made excellent use of my time working with Rose, but I knew that this latest scam came with a built-in expiration date. The line that I needed to walk to make sure that I extracted everything I could out of her was thin, because I had to take her actual failings into account as well. When she was legitimately short, I would have to forgo my usual exploitation to make sure that she was still around for the next opportunity. I began leaning harder on some of my bolder weekday methods and found myself becoming more comfortable with that process with every shift. My time in the office gave me even more of a peek behind the curtain than the audit had and provided confirmation that Big Brother wouldn't have been able to watch us if he'd actually cared to do so. The only limiting factor to consider was my conscience, which was already well into an extended leave of absence. Incidentally, Rose was actually relieved of her duties for a completely unrelated reason after a few months of our weekend mornings together. She picked the wrong time to not card a twenty-eight-year-old regular for his cigarette purchase.

Chapter Eighteen

While I became a cynic at a very young age, I also maintained an idealistic streak much longer than I liked to let on. I wanted so badly to believe that life was fair and people were good, and for the longest time, I acted as if that was the case in the face of all evidence to the contrary. I doubled down on the importance of concepts like honesty and industriousness and keeping my head down, long past the point where those strategies made sense. I developed a duality in the way I looked at the world and I learned to keep my mouth shut, as it became clear that the only thing people hated more than an ideological enemy was the individual who dared to take a more nuanced approach. I felt like I was a better person than everyone else, because I understood how valuable integrity should be and other people apparently did not. If the world had been collapsing, I had the audacity to believe that if only everyone thought the way I'd thought, everything would have been perfect for everyone all the time. I carried that self-righteous spark into my early twenties and while it still flickers to this day, my time at the gas station played a big part in nearly stamping it out.

***

I was never interested in learning the names of the vendors or making any small talk when they'd come into the store, but some didn't annoy me as much as others. If they came in and appeared focused on getting through the day, I would give them the benefit of the doubt. If they were loud or had a lot to say or just spent more than the minimum amount of time in the store, I considered them to have worn out their welcome. While I would never ask them to leave, I made it obvious that I had work to do and, thus, didn't have time to stand around and talk about the weather. I knew that any time that I spent behind the register that my job didn't require of me was time that I wasn't spending doing something more important, and I tried to indicate this. It wasn't my intention to be rude, and most of the vendors seemed to pick up on this aspect of my personality over time. I was fully aware that most of the vendors had jobs that were much more challenging than my own and I couldn't help but think that some of the quieter ones were dealing with a similar sort of garden-variety angst. Regarding the rest, I was under the impression that they were just as oblivious as everyone else that came in through the front door.

I suppose my favorite of the delivery men was the Frito-Lay vendor, who made two weekly stops. He looked like the mustachioed version of William H. Macy, was a fast worker, and would often lay the invoice on the counter without a word before heading back out to his truck. On one memorable morning, I was watching him run through his usual routine: removing the products that were out of date, replacing them with new packages, restocking those that sold, and finally rotating the oldest that were left to the front. While most of his best-selling items had space bought and paid for on the right side of the center rack, those with more of a niche appeal were relegated to hanging on metal clip strips placed in various out-of-the-way nooks and crannies. One such example was the six-and-a-half-ounce bag of Keebler Tato Skins. The Tato Skins were usually sold for ninety-nine cents, as indicated by the price stamped above each bag's sell-by date. They weren't a big seller, and so when I saw ol' Jerry Lundegaard take out his roll of bright orange stickers, it made pretty good sense. When he'd completed his task and moved out of the way, I'd finally been able to read the labels he had placed over the previously advertised price:

SALE!
$1.19

I had developed such contempt for everything involved with the store that finding the humor in it became necessary for my survival. I hated the company, I hated my coworkers, I hated the customers, and I hated myself. Any fleeting exceptions were immediately offset due to guilt by association. I hated the way that we ripped people off, and I hated the idea that the customers signed on for it. I hated my coworkers for their total lack of effort, and I hated myself for being stupid enough to continue picking up the slack. I hated the way that I hid behind my supposed intellect and virtue to ensure that I didn't have to try to do something better with my life. It was a toxic situation, and one could have made a good argument that my presence was the worst part of the whole thing. I was fully aware of that, and when that knowledge became too much to bear, I took it out on the customers and out of the register. As ridiculous as the whole situation was, I never gave leaving a second thought. After all, there was work to be done.

My favorite shifts were those during which the store became invisible to the general public. While it was true that I wouldn't have a job without the customers, the location of our store basically guaranteed that would never be a problem. Overnight allowed for quite a bit of downtime, but we still had enough pay-at-the-pump sales that the corporate office saw no reason to think about canceling the shift. Any time on the clock that didn't involve face-to-face interactions was as close to a blessing as I could imagine. After all, my least favorite part of working in customer service was the customer, followed closely by the service. I would have been game to hoist trash bags into the dumpster and scrub toilets for the rest of my life if it could guarantee me a living wage and a lack of customer contact, but I knew that wasn't going to happen. There would be no bathrooms to clean or garbage to handle without our patrons, but that didn't make me appreciate them more. It wasn't as if the company paid me more for dealing with more people or for collecting more cash for the store. Even after my recent promotion, after adjusting for inflation, quite the opposite was true.

The fall of 2006 saw me reach my fourth anniversary as an employee of Logic Oil Company. Before I received my promotion, I had received a twenty-five cent raise each year. The seventy-five-cent third shift premium or 'death bonus' tacked on to my base pay had brought my hourly wage up to the gaudy figure of $6.90 per hour. While it was the most money that I had ever made, it was only fifteen cents more than what I'd earned washing dishes in my hometown in the summer of 1999. We received word that the State of Michigan would be raising the minimum wage from $5.15 to $6.95 at the beginning of October, and then to $7.15 during the summer of 2007. While the cashiers were excited about the news, the same could not be said for the main office. I understood the corporate position, as such an increase in wages was going to have a considerable effect on the company's profit margin. Management let us know that yearly raises might not happen and that they might have to cut hours for those who were in non-essential roles. They made it clear that not a single person in the store was in an essential role.

I had my own reservations about the change, but my coworkers did not understand where I was coming from. They were confident that each cashier would somehow receive a raise equal to the initial one-dollar-and-eighty-cents bump in the minimum wage, but I knew that an unstated cap on our hourly rates would make that quite unlikely. I told them that they should only expect their pay to be raised to the new minimum wage, regardless of what they were already making. This suggestion was met with great resistance, and half of the staff said that they would immediately resign if that were the case. When the increase finally came through, it played out exactly as I'd thought it would. Some cashiers were happy with their arbitrary raises, and others were rightfully angry that new hires would be coming in at a rate of pay equal to their own, but no one ended up quitting. On my end, I was not at all surprised to see that I'd received a five-cent pay raise, the night shift premium now removed from my check, and no shift supervisor compensation in sight. By that time, it had long since stopped mattering to me.

Chapter Nineteen

About halfway through high school, I thought that I had developed a much better ability to deal with change than I had in the past. Gone were the temper tantrums and the absolute need to have everything spelled out for me—replaced by stoic resignation to the reality that there would be a lot of things that I wouldn't have the slightest hope of controlling. I enjoyed reveling in the idea that I was some sort of old soul who saw things for what they really were, but the first few years of adulthood wore me down and left me without any way to cope. The truth is that I never really learned how to handle anything, I didn't want to change, and I certainly didn't want to grow. I was reluctant because I had never seen any evidence that there was anything to gain from doing so—the results seemed arbitrary, at best. Edward Abbey said that growth for the sake of growth was only the ideology of a cancer cell, and that made perfect sense to me. The change would be the only constant, and personal growth was supposed to be the best way to deal with that, but this ideology led me to conclude that life was nothing but a terminal illness. This seemed like a pretty good cosmic joke, told by an extremely talented comedian. The best method I'd discovered for self-medicating my way through the human condition was to find humor wherever it could be found. Looking back, I realize I'd made the mistake of trying to treat the symptom rather than the disease.

***

In the first few months of her tenure as the store manager, Pam did little to change the way things ran. She didn't appear to be actively stealing and she didn't pay enough attention to notice when I did, so I got along with her as well as you could expect. She took her cigarette breaks seriously, and so you can imagine that she was popular with the other cashiers. Any addition by subtraction that the station would have seen following Paul's departure was minimized by Pam's deference to Donna, but I wasn't particularly concerned. As disjointed as it may have been, I was enjoying the way that my new schedule split up my week, primarily because it resulted in less store work getting done during routine daily operations. I liked watching the station's condition degrade because it made it easier to look like I was making headway when I was finally able to swoop in. In the ranking of soul-sucking tasks, the office work was somewhere between scrubbing the urinals and talking to the customers. If I couldn't be huffing homebrew mustard gas and making a real difference in the men's room, then attempting to balance the daily paperwork would have to suffice. It definitely beat the alternative.

When it was clear that Pam had become comfortable in her role, we started to see some things change. There was a marked attempt to hold people more accountable for their poor performance, but it was wasted due to the continued staff churn. Some cashiers received warnings and even formal write-ups, but their tendency to stop showing up for work at all meant that Pam didn't have many opportunities to make a real statement. By the time her schedule lined up with that of her disciplinary target, if the person hadn't moved on, a one-time incident was often too far in the past to warrant any follow-up. As a result, most of my coworkers started to see their work get nitpicked, with varying results. Some cashiers took it all in stride, others just nodded along, and it was widely accepted that Pam was looking for a target. While I managed to escape the unwanted attention—as Josh informed me one day during shift change—he was not so lucky.

"So, get this—I get in today, and Pam says we need to talk. Apparently, someone—I'm thinking Donna—saw me drink a quart of milk in the cooler the other day and told her that I didn't pay for it. That's one hundred percent true, but if she had done some research or maybe just asked me, she would have found out that it was expired. It was up for grabs. It has always been up for grabs. It's going down the drain, right? I tried to point that out to Pam, and I asked her if she really thought I would steal milk in front of the assistant manager. Do you know what she said?"

"Expired milk has never been up for grabs?" I guessed.

"No. Pam said that she didn't know me well enough to know that I wouldn't steal and that she had to trust her assistant manager. We went back and forth on the reasons she shouldn't do that for about fifteen minutes and long story short, I'm pretty sure they're going to fire me over a quart of milk."

"Wait, so—she's firing you on second-hand information from Donna? Does she know about the lizard problem?"

"She does now. But hey, those are two separate issues, and one has no bearing on the level of trust she should place in the woman, right? They're not going to end up firing me, though. I'm just going to turn in my shirt before my shift tomorrow."

"I thought you were the one that Donna liked, though?"

"Yeah, so did I," said Josh.

"Well, I mean... what if you just ask her what's up? There's really nothing to lose since you're planning on quitting. I'd be curious to hear how she spins it."

"I just wonder why she didn't tell her about the sandwich— that wasn't even expired! I guess we'll never know," said Josh, laughing as he headed back up to the platform.

"Oh man, haha. Yeah, I guess it doesn't matter since you're leaving anyway."

"Oh no, I'd definitely stop in to talk to her about it, but…"

I gave Josh what had become my customary look in these situations.

"Oh, yeah, you had two days off, so you don't know, do you?"

"Nope."

"Donna quit. She's moving back to Weidman," said Josh, referencing a tiny village located about twenty-five miles southwest of Mount Pleasant.

"I thought she was from Edmore?"

"Oh yeah, big difference there. Anyway, I guess she's tired of the drive."

"Doesn't Crystal drive in from like forty-five miles, though?" I responded.

"Yeah, but she's got kids to feed, and the old man works in town, too," said Josh.

"When he works, sure."

Josh laughed the way that people do when they're happy to have set someone up to deliver a punchline. I wasn't ready for him to move on, but I had known that it was coming for some time. He was graduating soon and most likely moving off somewhere that was much less of a cultural wasteland. I was going to miss our conversations, as I hadn't found anyone I connected with for a long time, but I was ultimately happy for him, and I was more than a little envious. Things were still wide open for him, and they felt narrow and shut for me.

"Alright, before I go," Josh said, "I'm going to tell you something, and you can do what you will with the information, but I want to hear the fallout from it if you decide to pass it on."

"Hmm… Twenty questions, then?"

"Something like that, sure."

"Paul was about to get fired for stealing?"

"Well, yeah, but that's not it," said Josh, laughing at the verbalization of the store's worst kept secret.

"Donna was in on it?"

"Well, of course, why else would she have turned him in first?"

"Morgan was dealing weed out of the store?"

"Haha, how did you hear all of this stuff working nights?"

"Crystal talks a lot of shit. I figure a third of it is true."

"Did she tell you that Paul was gay?"

"No, haha," I said, laughing.

"Well, I guess he is now, according to the dude from Advanced Employment," said Josh.

"Jason?"

"Yeah, that sounds right."

"Well, right on."

"Bully for him," said Josh.

"A credible source on that one, too. Was that it?" I asked.

"No, haha. This is going to blow your mind, though."

Once again, I gave Josh a look that gave him the option to continue if he felt it was going to be worth my while. He continued.

"Alright, so, I saw Rose at Meijer a while back, and we were talking about Donna. I mentioned that I almost had the... misfortune... of seeing her doing her thing with some random trucker right after I started."

"Oh, Jesus. No wonder you left the first time."

"Ha, it gets better, though. Rose did her one-upper thing with me," said Josh.

"Oh yeah?"

"Yeah. You know how she'd come in like two hours early, just to read the paper in the back?"

"Yes, of course."

"Well, I don't think Donna expected that when she filled in on nights. So, Rose shows up one morning, pulls the car around the back, and sees Donna out there with—you ready for this?"

"If it's the lady with the Taz shirt, I'm going to be very upset."

"Haha, oh, Jesus... No, but that's a good guess. Rose actually saw Donna out back with The Intimidator, himself."

Josh continued to speak, but at that point, I was more concerned with processing what I had heard, so I couldn't tell you what other details he shared. I wasn't surprised to hear the old man had cheated on Crystal, but I couldn't understand why he would choose to do so with someone like Donna. He had some knowledge of how to attract younger and better-looking women, and Donna seemed like an age-appropriate step down that he would have been unwilling to take. I briefly entertained the idea that they had hit upon some sort of special connection, but I knew enough about both of them to understand that was most likely not the case. They had almost certainly just conducted a business deal, one of many that Donna was rumored to be involved in every week. I found myself weighing the relative merits of telling Crystal what I had heard and trying to stay out of things that weren't my business. It wasn't as if telling her was going to result in her leaving the old man and falling into my arms on the rebound. In the end, I decided that I didn't want to get any more involved. It wasn't my place to speak, and the low-rent soap opera would work itself out one way or another.

"Well... alright," I said.

"Yeah, that's pretty much what I said, too."

"Alright, so—I have some questions."

"Me too, but none that I want answered."

"How about this? Maybe you can help with this one," I said.

"I'll see what I can do, but if this is a question about the logistics…"

"Oh god. No, this is much more important," I said.

"Hit me," said Josh, expectantly.

"Are you still going to pick me up for work?"

Chapter Twenty

The six weeks following Josh's second escape passed quickly. I was so entrenched in my routine that I was living on autopilot and thus I was as content as I could reasonably expect to be. With my schedule set and the busiest part of the year over and nothing on the horizon, the days and weeks and months and seasons started to matter less and less. I was collecting paychecks and supplementing them with at least twenty-five dollars in "found money" every night. Almost all of the food I ate came off the racks at the store, and to escape suspicion, I made the effort to be seen paying for something during every shift. On the last day of my work week, I would make sure to take home enough fine cuisine to make it all the way to my Thursday-night substitute-Monday. When I grew tired of guzzling free tap water at home, I'd make my way to the station to abuse the free fountain pop policy. As a result of all this penny pinching and dollar grifting, I started to accumulate a bit of a nest egg. When it exceeded five thousand dollars, I thought that it might be time to move it out of the junk drawer and into a more secure place. While there were plenty of things that I needed—dependable transportation, most of all—I couldn't bring myself to actually spend very much of the money. I had worked too hard for it.

The more routine that my life became, the more I found that I was able to coast through it without my thoughts getting in the way. I was still filled with the same self-doubt and hatred for my position and place, but I was settling into a comfortably apathetic state. I let my guard down and was able to relate more and more with my coworkers and the customers, and I didn't let the assimilation bother me like I had in the past. With the example of Josh gone and my interactions with Crystal now tainted by a pattern of deceit by omission, I knew my standards for decency were falling by the wayside. I was a happier person than I had been in some time, but I felt less like myself than I'd ever felt. In my youth, I would have railed against that sort of unearned contentedness, but I didn't seem to have it in me anymore. The initial rush of pride that I had felt after finally taking back something for myself had long since run out. I wasn't any different than anyone else, and I realized how little any of it actually mattered. I just smiled and tried to embrace my descent further into the land of small minds and small talk.

***

"So, if most of the money you make comes from tips, what happens when you don't get scheduled to work one of the big nights of the week?"

"It doesn't make a difference to me. I make two hundred dollars in tips on a Tuesday night, motherfucker," said Rachel, perhaps the closest that I had to a favorite regular.

"Two hundred dollars, Jesus."

"Pretty much, and if not, there's always going to be a high roller on one of the slow nights who'll get me caught up."

"So those guys are pretty much always there, then?"

"Some, but there are also a lot of random dudes showing off for their buddies."

"Ah, that makes sense."

"Yeah, it does."

"Okay, there it is—one-oh-five on the pop. Any chips or candy tonight?"

"Do you see them up here?"

"Nope, but you know…"

"Yep, I know. Alright, sweetie, have a great night."

"You too. Thanks, and see you next time."

I watched Rachel walk all the way back to her car, and in the interest of not letting her know how creepy I was acting, I made sure to avert my gaze before she turned to enter the vehicle. Two hundred dollars in tips seemed like a ridiculous amount to bring in on a Tuesday night, but it wasn't implausible given what she was working with. I didn't think it was likely that any of the other women at the casino were making that kind of money, based on what I had seen from them at the store. They may have been more skilled, but for the most part, they were lacking in the most essential qualifications for the position. I was thinking about how impressive Rachel's curriculum vitae was when I headed out the front door to take care of the outside trash. Once I reached the receptacle farthest from the entrance, a burgundy Buick Skylark rolled into the lot and—predictably—came to a stop in front of the prominent No Parking sign. This was such a common occurrence that I would sometimes crack a joke about the first word having worn off of the sign, but no one had ever called me out on it. No one had ever laughed, either.

Out of reflex, I dropped what I was doing and made a mad dash back to my post. In most cases, the customer would enter the store before I could get behind the register, but this time, the man decided to finish smoking his cigarette. The man's refusal to follow our admittedly arbitrary rules annoyed me, but I chose not to mention that his vehicle was blocking my line of sight. I also decided not to let him know that we didn't allow smoking within ten feet of the building, because I didn't see what good might come of it. As the customer didn't seem to be in a hurry, I went to the back room and grabbed two more bundles of paper towels so that I could fill the outside dispensers when he left. When I returned to the front, I saw that he had entered the store and was already at the counter with a twenty-ounce bottle of Mountain Dew. I suggested that he might want some chips or candy to go with his beverage, and he declined and instead asked for a hard pack of Newports. I rang him up, recited the rest of the script, performed the transaction, and sent him on his way.

When the man left the store, I noticed that one of our fuel drivers had pulled into the diesel pumps out back for his nightly fill-up. I waited for him to take the nozzle off of the cradle, approved the pump, and headed back outside. Rather than immediately leave the premises, the previous customer opted to hang around and smoke his second cigarette in the last five minutes. I glanced back up at him after every trash can, and I wasn't surprised to see that he was not in much of a hurry to get anywhere. After all, the 2:00 AM cutoff for alcohol sales had already passed. When he finished his smoke, I once again had to cut my work short and sprint back in to assume my post. My attempted upsell may not have worked in the moment, but it had apparently stuck with the smoking man, as he was already contemplating the chip rack by the time I made it onto the platform. Seconds later, I heard the tell-tale whistling of Doug the fuel driver as he entered the station and headed to the sink to rinse out his company-branded coffee mug. He would only ever whistle two certain songs—neither of which I could identify—but his choice seemed to depend on the weather.

The repeat customer made his way to the till with a bag of Flamin' Hot Cheetos, which seemed like a pretty decent pairing for his previously purchased beverage. I ran through the President's Club script again, knowing full well how rehearsed it would sound to a man who had heard it less than five minutes prior. I got a kick out of the absurdity of running through the stilted and transparent line of questioning with no thought given to the way that my words were being received. He didn't seem to be amused or bothered—just quiet, and the slightest bit more stoned than sober. He had not said more than two words since the time he arrived, and my preconceptions about his ethnicity made me think that he might not be particularly confident in the use of English. I had just rung up his selection and told him his total when he finally spoke again and cleared up the confusion.

"Money. Give me the money," he said calmly.

I heard what he had said, but I didn't process it until I looked down and saw that he had produced a gun from his track pants. My first reaction upon seeing the weapon was to laugh, but not out of any sort of nervous anxiety. In reality, the man was attempting to rob me with what I know now to be a replica of Wyatt Earp's ivory-handled Colt Cavalry Model Single Action revolver, shined to the point that it looked to have never been drawn from a holster. It was a strange choice of firearm for someone who wasn't a time traveler. I had always known that I would get robbed, but I usually pictured the weapon as a butterfly knife or a sawed-off shotgun or the traditional sideways held 9mm Glock pistol. Nevertheless, I had to assume that the gun was loaded and that the man was prepared to use it. I had already begun asking him to repeat himself before I felt a delayed surge of fight-or-flight hormones released into my bloodstream. I knew exactly what he had said, but it still didn't stop the words from coming out of my mouth.

"I'm sorry, what was that?"

"The money. Give me the money," he said, much less calmly.

I popped open the register by inserting the broken key into the keyhole, joining it with the stuck other half and turning it counterclockwise. The till opened and I once again had to hold back a chuckle, as the drawer was almost entirely devoid of bills that did not feature the face of our nation's first president. I had recently done a safe drop, and the cash that I had left in the drawer had been immediately erased by the somewhat rare occurrence of two consecutive customers who carried nothing but one-hundred-dollar bills. I gathered the remaining cash—including the two ones in the money clip alarm, just for Crystal—and gave the man his money. I made a quick attempt to commit the face to memory and read his license plate as he bolted out the door, and it was then that I noticed that our height chart actually started six inches off of the ground. It shouldn't surprise you to learn that I made sure to thank the man and tell him that I would see him next time, all before the door had shut. I wasn't going to let something as insignificant as an armed robbery stop me from continuing to earn my special polo shirt and the matching winter jacket that I would never wear.

Chapter Twenty-One

This actually wasn't the first time the store was robbed under my watch, but it was the first time that had involved a weapon. The case could be made that a robbery took place any time that Paul was allowed near the till or an even better one in light of my own recent behavior. If you wanted to expand the definition, you could count dozens of successful drive-offs over the years under the same banner, as well. However, my favorite example happened very early in my tenure, at the hands of what you might best describe as a transient gentleman. He had walked across the street from the McDonald's parking lot and asked if he could pay with a fifty-dollar bill. I sold him a pack of Camel Lights in a soft pack and had started to make the change from a ten-dollar bill when he promptly leaped across the counter and grabbed three twenties out of the drawer. He left the same way he had come and disappeared into the night—I hadn't even gotten a chance to see him make his getaway. After calling the police, filing a report, and having a grainy photo run in the newspaper the next day, he was brought to justice. I later learned that his drug dealer had decided that his tab was past due, so he stole a friend's car and made the twenty-five-mile trek from Barryton into the big city in an attempt to get together enough cash to settle up. He was actually turned in by his church pastor and served three months in jail. I still think that he made the right choice, given the situation.

During the half decade that I had worked at the store, I hadn't heard of a single gas station in town getting held up at gunpoint. As rough as the economy was, it seemed like we should have seen more of that type of crime, but that was not the case. The robber's showpiece revolver was the first handgun that I had ever seen that wasn't on the belt of a member of law enforcement at the time. As much of a bubble as Mid Michigan could be, the people I was exposed to while working overnight made it clear that something was eventually going to happen. There was too much stupidity and there were too many drugs. I'd never trusted many people in the first place and getting to know what the general public was all about hadn't changed that for the better. After factoring in the continuing atrophy of my own ethical framework, I still didn't feel like I would have something coming back at me, but I definitely had gained a better understanding of human nature than ever before. Given over a thousand nights that I would spend at the store, knowing that I would have a gun in my face sooner or later was just a matter of playing the odds—it was a pretty safe bet.

***

After the robber had made his getaway, I turned to Doug, who had taken a longer time at the sink than necessary.

"Please lock that door," I directed him.

"Did we just get robbed?"

"Yes. I'll get the other one. Please lock that door."

"Alright, alright. Now what?"

"Now we call Central Dispatch and wait for the cops."

"Did you get it on video?"

"Yeah, we should definitely have him on the tape. He came into the store twice and walked around, so we have like five minutes of footage from a few different angles."

"Did you recognize him? How much did he get?"

"Not at all. I think he probably got about fifty bucks. Did you see the gun?"

"Fifty bucks! That's not even wo—wait, he had a gun?"

"Well, yeah."

"Really?"

"Well, did you think he was going to use his finger, genius?"

"Haha... No, it's just... it's... it's freakin' Mount Pleasant."

Human beings often display a fascinating lack of awareness about things that are taking place right under their noses. We can travel all over the world and become verifiable experts in all manner of things without ever learning about our surroundings, our neighbors, or even ourselves. To put it bluntly, we don't know what we don't know. In Doug's case, no matter how many times I told him about the seedy underbelly of Mount Pleasant, he was just as flabbergasted as he was the first time that I told him all about those little glass tubes. I can only imagine what he might have thought if I ever told him about that old farmhouse out there on River Road. As for myself, I had long since become immune to surprise. I was just as likely to wonder why it took so long for humanity to sink to the next level as I was to shake my head at the absurdity. Every step further down the spiral seemed like yet another toward the logical conclusion of absolute foolishness. I didn't exclude my own actions from that judgment.

Sergeant Stephen Black of the Michigan State Police pulled into the parking lot in his blue Crown Victoria and approached the door, pen and paper in hand, less than five minutes after I made my call to Central Dispatch. Sergeant Black had pulled me over several times, and he had responded to my occasional drive-off report, so I wasn't unfamiliar with him. He was a Marine, which showed in his demeanor, but he had also mastered the art of channeling that intensity into a more welcoming energy that was somehow even more overbearing and exhausting. He was there to protect and serve, but if you happened to stand in the way of him doing that, he might run right over you. For lack of a better description, he was an aggressively nice man. I had run into guys like him in the past and they had always rubbed me the wrong way, but the fact that he carried a gun and a billy club made it easy for me to refrain from voicing my distaste through the usual clever wordplay and snide commentary. Even so, it was all I could do not to laugh out loud when he attempted to fling open the deadbolted door and met the full resistance of the entire building. Rather than let him succeed in taking the door off of the hinge, I opted to meet him halfway.

"Hello. Sergeant Stephen Black," he said, extending his hand for what would be a cartoonishly firm handshake, and apparently forgetting that he had introduced himself to me in the same way on no less than ten separate occasions.

"Hello."

"We're going to get this taken care of for you, but before I go any further, could I get your full name?"

"James Jonathan Sims," I said.

"Common spelling of James?" asked Sergeant Black.

"I... yeah... common spelling," I answered, dumbfounded.

"What is your current address, Mr. Sims?"

"One zero seven four nine Chippewa Road, Lot forty-two, Mount Pleasant. Zip is four—"

"Thank you, Jim. Can I call you Jim?"

"I don't see why not, sure."

"Let's just go with James, Jim."

"Alright, that works."

"Well James, what exactly happened here?"

I explained the events, from the interruption of my duties to the disregard for the No Parking sign to the cigarettes to the initial transaction before finally leading up to the robbery. As I told the story, I noticed that Sergeant Black was able to take long-form notes faster than I would be able to take shorthand. When I got to the part of the story where it was time to describe the perpetrator, I could almost see the lightbulb go on above the officer's head. He asked if he could have access to our security camera footage, so I headed back to the office to begin tracking down the sixty-second incident. In the meantime, Sergeant Black took a witness statement from Doug, who seemed like he was just happy to be involved in something straight out of the small-town evening news. I couldn't imagine that he would have much to say about the event, given the fact that he didn't turn around for one second while it occurred, but that didn't stop him from talking Sergeant Black's ear off.

When Logic Oil Company had originally purchased the surveillance system, it was very likely the state of the art. With four cameras set to continuously record both audio and video and only minimal opportunity for user error each day, I have no doubt that the company had invested a large sum of money and received a considerable discount on insurance when they had it installed. However, I am also confident that there have been many advances in the technology over the twenty years that had passed, and it was evident that they had all been completely ignored. The videocassette recorder was set up so that it could record twenty-four hours of video on one six-hour tape, and the number of tapes on hand dictated that we could archive nearly a full month's worth of footage. I've come to learn that most businesses do not hold on to their recordings for nearly that long, but on the night of the robbery, I also came to understand that recording over the same videocassette tapes dozens of times can produce some pretty interesting analog artifacts. Viewing the footage of the robbery was a sort of out-of-body experience, with my corporeal form splitting up duties with transparent apparitions of those from my past. I had a laugh when I was struck with the thought that the ghost images weren't getting any less work done than I was earlier in the night.

It took me about ten minutes to track down the first appearance of the perpetrator. Due to the condition of the tape, I had to rely on the timestamp to be sure that I was looking at the right person. There were so many other faded faces and bodies that the only person identifiable on the tape was me. It didn't bode well for using the video for any sort of blown-up footage as zooming in would only serve to further degrade the image. I was inching through the encounter frame by frame and looking in vain for a clear picture of the assailant when Sergeant Black came back to the office to check into my progress. When I showed him the condition of the recording, he didn't seem fazed. While it looked like a dead end to me, the officer was oddly confident that his team would find a usable image. His confidence didn't make a lot of sense given the low-resolution, three-quadrant mess displayed on the tiny monochrome screen in the office. He told me that he was going to complete his report and that he would be back for the tape, so I locked the door behind him and got back to work.

As I finished overstocking the plastic straws, I heard the tell-tale sound of the irresistible force once again attempting to move the immovable object. When I headed over to unlock the door, Doug beat me to the punch. Sergeant Black walked toward me with real purpose before stopping at a distance that was somehow equally commanding and reassuring. He reached inside his Moleskine notebook and inexplicably produced a small, full-color mugshot of the man who had robbed the store.

The date and timestamp on the photo indicated that it had been printed just four hours earlier, so I had first assumed that the clock on the squad car's mobile printer must have been set incorrectly. I noticed that the perpetrator was also wearing the exact same outfit he had worn when he was in the store earlier in the evening. While it wasn't out of the question for anyone to be wearing the same shirt in two different pictures and could almost be considered likely in the case of the trash that I dealt with on a night-to-night basis, Sergeant Black must have sensed my attempt at rationalizing what I was seeing. He took the opportunity to speak.

"Mr. Sims, first things first—I wanted to apologize for cutting you off earlier. I should have let you recite your zip code. I assumed that I knew it, but you're close enough to the county line that there's a chance that I could have been wrong."

"No worries, Sergeant Black. It didn't mean that much to me. It's four, eight, eight, five, eight."

"I know it is, Jim."

I smiled, but the smile gave away to a smirk.

"Mr. Sims, we picked this gentleman up earlier this evening when the mother of his child called nine-one-one to let us know that he had threatened her while he was drunk. We didn't have any evidence of it going any further than that, but he resisted, and so we took him in. Obviously, his lawyer got him out of there pretty quick. Personally, I don't know how far he would have gotten with the lady based on the fact that that he's the one with scratches on his face, and I think there might be more going on there than a few drinks. I have a few other pictures we can go through, but I wanted to ask you first. Is this the man you saw, and if so, would you be comfortable identifying him in a lineup?"

There wasn't a single thing about what Sergeant Black had said that didn't make perfect sense based on what I had come to learn about people during my time at the store. The idea of a local guy getting drunk and maybe smoking some meth, threatening his girlfriend, getting manhandled by her, and then heading out to rob a gas station with an antique revolver somehow seemed to be nothing more than par for the course. That was definitely not the case for Doug. I could see that the twenty years he had on me had done nothing to open his mind to the world of extreme possibilities. I found it strange that a man who had grown up in Mt. Pleasant and had worked in so many blue-collar jobs was still capable of being surprised by a little low-level degeneracy, but he was dumbfounded. He stood there with his mouth agape, taking it in and almost certainly trying to commit the story to memory for his buddies. The officer scrawled the case number of his police report on a business card, which I would eventually paperclip to my shift report to explain my cash shortage, as denoted by the following line in the register's ending totals:

(ROBBERY) Paid Out: $42.00

SERVICE

Chapter Twenty-Two

When I came in for my next shift, I was greeted by the sight of a "new" cathode-ray terminal hanging near the register for all to see, displaying the feed from the relic that was our security system. While most modern systems tended to display video in an ultra-crisp greyscale, our combination of compromised components of questionable quality properly presented life at the convenience store as more of a muddled mess. Nevertheless, it did not stop customers from taking in the glory of their own foggy and pixelated projections and presumably wondering if they might actually be watching *Pickard Shell's Greatest Hits, 1980-1984*. Crystal was behind the register looking unimpressed as she entertained what passed for conversation with the small group of gawking onlookers. I offered her the only sort of smile that one could offer when coming in to work the night shift at a gas station less than twenty-four hours after getting robbed while doing the same. She did her best to return the favor with the only proper response. For a girl that was usually so animated, she was able to throw on a very convincing and restrained 'white-people smile' when the situation called for it.

"That's gotta make you feel safer," said one of the three customers.

"Shit, no—if it's gonna happen, it's gonna happen. Crazy people don't care about no video," said Crystal.

"Well, at least they'll catch them when it happens," said the second customer.

"Sure. That's not going to do me much good when I'm bleeding out, but yeah, the company might get their money back," I interjected.

Crystal laughed.

"Oh my god, don't say that shit," said Crystal.

"What, you don't you want them to get caught?"

"Haha. No, I get it, but what if it that ends up happening now?"

"Then it happens, I guess."

"Only 'cause you put it out there," said Crystal.

"Well, I guess I can't prove that wouldn't be the case," I conceded.

"See?"

She appeared to have a point, but she didn't.

"Wait, though. We just went from 'if it's gonna happen, it's gonna happen' to voodoo?"

"Whatever, dude, you should know better by now."

She was right. I definitely should have known better by then. I definitely should have known better than to have become interested in her in the first place. It wasn't so much because she was out of my league, as that had never stopped me in the past. But more so because I shouldn't have ever given her a second thought, and I never would have if not for the proximity effect. In short, she was the only semi-attractive woman with whom I had regular contact, and that compelled me to romanticize the things I didn't hate about her and write off the things I did as endearing quirks and cute idiosyncrasies. My attempts at a love life were littered with these sorts of questionable infatuations, particularly with girls who seemed hell bent to end up either the victim or instigator in a relationship built on a foundation of emotional abuse. I wasn't enough of the kind of asshole that could keep a woman like that interested, but I was too much of another type of asshole to attract the women that I wanted. Rather than set my sights on trying to better myself, I settled for crushing on girls like Crystal, if for no other reason than because they were always there—simple props to occupy my time.

When the store cleared out and we finished with the shift change, Crystal assumed her post outside the door and began her usual ritual. I didn't have it in me to make a wisecrack about smoking while pregnant, because I couldn't honestly say that I cared what happened with her kids one way or the other. I had more of a problem with what her smoking was doing to her looks, but there wasn't any point to saying anything about that because she had recently taken to preempting any and all advice with her own harsh self-judgment. She was aging before her time and before my eyes. She didn't seem to be as amused by her struggles as she had when I first met her. She was doubling down on negativity and almost daring me to try to make her laugh. At times, she had the perfect comeback chambered for any sunshine or mirth or words of encouragement that anyone might try to bring into her life; and I could tell that this would be one of those times. She was getting so invested in her depression and making such a hobby out of her anxiety that any help a sane person might want to offer would likely not be out of empathy but out of a desire to shut her the fuck up.

That said, it probably wouldn't surprise you to learn that I still thought it was my responsibility to try to fix her problems. It didn't matter how many times I was told not to do that, because I knew that any restraint I might show could be interpreted as a lack of concern. The situation was nothing more than a trap, and I knew that the best policy would be to disengage, but I just couldn't do it. The inclusion of human nature on either side of an equation had always given me fits because I didn't actually relate to anyone. I would try to imagine myself in the position of the other and think about how I would want to be treated. In this instance and most others, this strategy meant that I would default to complete honesty. With that in mind, I decided that I would tell Crystal everything I knew about Donna and the old man, and the sooner, the better. Eleven o'clock on a Monday night was as good a time as you could ever ask for to deliver bad news. It could have been any time, though—it wasn't like it would ever be any easier.

Given the nature of the news, I waited until Crystal had started her second post-shift cigarette before I dropped what I was doing to talk to her.

"So..."

If nothing else, I always knew how to get a conversation off to an awkward start.

"So what?"

"So—there's something I wanted to talk to you about," I said.

"Oh, dude, I'm sorry, but I don't like you like that," said Crystal, laughing.

I knew she was joking with me, but I was also aware that she was telling the truth.

"Seriously, though," I said.

"Oh, Jesus, what's up?" said Crystal, obviously already a bit on edge.

"First of all, I don't really have proof of this, but I feel like I shoul—"

"You wanna talk some shit?"

"Seriously, Crystal," I said, attempting to keep the conversation on track.

"Okay, dude, we'll talk some serious shit. I'll go first."

"Fine."

"He said 'fine' like a teenage girl, Jesus."

"Alright. Go on. Go first."

"Oh, yes sir! Alright, check this out—you already know I'm pregnant, right?"

"Yep, you're definitely in the family way."

"So that's awesome, right? But guess what's even better?"

If nothing else, Crystal seemed to be intent on providing me with plenty of opportunities for taking control of the conversation. I decided not to take any of them, as I was curious about what she might tell me. We shared a common quirk in the way we dealt with bad news in that we couldn't help but turn it into a joke, but I'd never received news that was as objectively horrible as what I planned on telling her. The longer our conversation went, the more nerve that I would lose, and the risk that I wouldn't get around to the whole reason that I was talking to her was very real. I prepared for Crystal to tell me about a reduction in her food stamps due to making too much money or something like that and I hoped that whatever she had to say might top what I was going to say, but I knew that wasn't going to be the case. I was getting a bit lost in thought when Crystal's measured voice snapped me back to reality.

"Hey. Jim. Guess what's even better?"

"I don't know, Crystal, what's even better?"

"Jesus, dude, play along. Guess."

I took a deep breath as she waited for my response. I wasn't even sure how to say it, so I ended up saying the first thing that came to mind.

"Crystal, the old man is cheating on you."

"What? Holy shit, dude, how long have you known?"

"I'm sorry, Crystal, I rea—"

"Oh fuck that, I've known forever. I want to know how long you've known. And stop saying my name every other fuckin' sentence."

I decided to lie to her. "I actually just heard it from Josh today."

"What? How the fuck would Josh know? He lives in Mount Pleasant."

"Well, I think he said he heard from someone else."

"Oh, whatever, he was just talkin' shit. That's a lucky guess, though."

There was a bit of uncomfortable and essential silence.

"So, what are you going to do?"

"Well, what the fuck am I supposed to do? I'm five months pregnant, we already have a kid together, and then there's his kids."

"There are options, though, aren't there?"

"Pshhh... not for me."

"What do you mean?"

She paused, and—for the first time I'd ever seen—displayed actual human vulnerability.

"I should have known though, look at me."

"Oh, what do you mean by that? It's not like he's cheating with someone who's better looking than you. I mean, not even close. He's just doing what assholes do."

She performed a sort of visible reset, wiping away the remnants of a few tears before going back on the offensive with her usual attack.

"You haven't even seen her, so save it. You don't even know what you're talking about, and you're just trying to make me feel better, and it's not going to fucking work. And thanks, by the way."

"For?"

"For telling me that I have shitty taste in men. Like I really fuckin' needed you to remind me of that."

Just like that, Crystal was out the door and into the night—done talking to me, at least for the time being. I watched her walk westward down Pickard, disappearing beneath the overpass, and I started to put two and two together. It sounded like she was more aware than any of us were that the old man was running around on her—quite possibly with someone that she felt she couldn't compete with. I suppose it shouldn't have surprised me that she would be aware of his proclivities, given their age difference. However, I don't think she had any idea that the father of her child was also compensating Donna for personal services rendered right there in the store's parking lot. I had done my part in trying to bring it up, but she had not allowed me to drive the point home the way that I had wanted to. It sounded like she'd made some strange sort of peace with the idea that he was cheating on her with a newer model, but I didn't think she would be able to do the same when she learned what was going on with Donna. Crystal took her money—as nonexistent as it was—as seriously as a twenty-four-year-old, chain-smoking lottery-addict who was supporting an unemployed, forty-year-old man and four kids ever could.

Chapter Twenty-Three

Despite how much she valued her earnings, Crystal ended up quitting the next day without giving notice. Due to the circumstances, I came in to relieve Pam after the second half of a double shift. When she told me that I'd be training Crystal's replacement on books the very next weekend, I couldn't help but let out an audible groan. Not a single other employee could be trusted in the office—even before factoring in the general lack of ability to complete the basic daily paperwork. Pam was pretty quick to attempt to ease my mind by letting me know that they had hired a college girl into Crystal's old assistant manager position. I briefly considered whether I would be justified in getting angry about that, but I chose to assume that the new girl was more qualified than me. This was an over-diplomatic conclusion, as Pam later informed me that the girl had never had a job before, but she had a "really great feeling about her." It made sense. My entire time at the store had been a comedy of errors and there was no reason to expect that to change. So I did my best to move on from the latest injustice and keep pushing forward—it didn't take long. There were cans of chew to pick up from the floor after the latest in a long line of attempts to fill the rack's broken center slot. There would always be more comedy, and there would always be more errors. There would always be more than enough pointless busy work to drown out the voice of reason in my head.

I had no downtime during that evening's shift. As classes at the university wouldn't start until the following Monday, nothing stood in the way for the college students that had already made their way back of spending the entire weekend getting hammered all over town. Thursday Night Happy Hour had always been just a way for them to pregame for Friday, and Saturday night was a runway that extended into Sunday—and sometimes Monday. Between the return of the kids and the late summer pull of the casino, I was well aware of what was in store for me that particular weekend. The more time that I spent trying to do my job meant the less time that I had to spend thinking about it, and that served as an adequate distraction from any possible moments of clarity that may have found their way into my consciousness. If I didn't want to risk making a bad situation worse, I couldn't afford to see things as they were for too long at any one time. I had already had enough so many times without doing anything about it and had come through the other side still in one piece that I had become acutely aware that such a melodramatic approach was nothing but histrionic posturing. I wasn't going anywhere.

When I arrived to train Lisa that Saturday morning, I narrated my actions while running through the standard shift change protocol. We were relieving the latest in a string of interchangeable overnight cashiers that never worked out, and it was just as well that I didn't remember his name because I'm sure it wasn't worth remembering. As for Lisa, she was your basic intelligent, midwestern college girl. She didn't seem like the type to join a sorority, but she also wasn't going to be showing up at Freak Night at the local meat-market college nightclub. She was pretty but downplayed it, and she probably had a steady but outclassed boyfriend with whom she was perfectly happy. I imagined that she ran track and played some basketball in high school but not well enough to earn a scholarship or walk on at the university. She seemed very grounded and struck me as the type of girl that was going to get her degree, get married, and find a good job in short order before settling down to raise a family right there in Mid Michigan. I couldn't imagine her venturing out past Grand Rapids, and the truth was that such a city would be the perfect size for her. I didn't find her interesting, we had nothing in common, and by the end of her first hour, it was clear that she was the most pleasant person I would ever work with at the store.

Since I had to run the register first and train Lisa second, she ended up spending the bulk of her first day waiting for me to return to the office and perform the next step in what was usually a two-and-a-half-hour process. We only opened up one register, and the volume of customers combined with the trainee's complete lack of experience meant that it was much more efficient if I handled all of the transactions for the first part of the day. When we entered the last two hours of the shift and had finished the books, it was time for Lisa to become acquainted with the register. The store traffic dropped to a manageable level, and I was able to cover all of the intricate workings of the VeriFone Ruby system. Lisa seemed to be genuinely excited to be there, and I did what I could not to spoil that for her. I didn't tell her about how the regular cashiers created more problems than they solved. I didn't tell her about how that they provided those of us making fifty cents more an hour with a never-ending procession of loose ends to tie up, all of which actually fell under the umbrella of their job descriptions. Looking back, I suppose that I could have told the truth because her demeanor was such that it wouldn't have deterred her from doing her best work in the slightest. I don't think she was that rational.

***

The limited training period meant that I had to let Lisa try her hand at the books the next morning, and she was very much up to the challenge. She'd taken pretty meticulous notes on that first day, but I never saw her refer to them once. Sometimes she took a little longer between tasks than I thought necessary, but that was expected given her lack of experience and my own penchant for completing useless mental math ahead of schedule. She had a better grasp of accounting than I ever did, and it didn't hurt that she had proper adding machine skills, either. When she would run into a dead end, she would immediately recognize and disclose her mistake before starting over from the beginning of that step. I didn't see her make any version of the same error twice. To compare her style with that of Donna was to know the difference between learning a skill and memorizing a task. My own method was somewhere between the two, and I never gave much thought to anything but that which made the least common sense. I enjoyed the pointlessness inherent in the undeniable madness of the supposed method, but Lisa seemed to have a passion for making sure that things came out right. It was clear from that day that she was beyond her position and place, but she still managed to do her job while coming across as both gracious and sincere.

With my questionable expertise not required in the office, I decided that there were more useful ways to spend my shift. It was the slowest of Sundays that I could remember and after taking care of the customer-centric cleaning tasks, I had enough time to run through each of the first-shift-specific tasks that hadn't been completed overnight. Between the laziness of the placeholder clerk and the traffic from the casino, it came as no surprise when I opened up the fake cappuccino machine and found that it had not been cleaned since my last night shift. The level of grime wasn't any worse than usual, but I knew that the machines hadn't been cleaned because I had placed the clipped corner of a bag of powdered drink mix underneath the Dutch Hot Cocoa container, and it had not been removed. In fact, it was covered by the same half-caramelized corn syrup mess that coated the rest of the inside of the machine. This was yet another way for me to collect irrefutable proof that I was a better worker than the other cashiers—information that I would only ever use to make myself feel good about my level of dedication to something so marginally important. After I cleaned and sanitized the stained and brittle plastic and rubber parts, I reassembled the machine and headed back to the office to check on Lisa.

When I got there, Lisa was correcting the previous day's mistakes on the cigarette inventory sheet. I hadn't shown her how, but it wasn't the most challenging set of calculations to reverse engineer from the numbers at hand. Rather than interrupt, I took a cursory glance at her progress on the rest of the day's paperwork. As far as weekend days went, Saturday had been a standard day for the store. We'd sold over three thousand gallons of gasoline, which translated to over nine thousand dollars in fuel sales. We'd managed to sell fifteen hundred dollars of store merchandise, and the day's safe drops had finished just short of seven thousand dollars in cash. Lisa took me up on the offer to take care of the bundling of the bills, and I dutifully did so in the same pattern that I had been half-shown by Donna. We had run out of five-dollar wrappers, so I was forced to use a jumbo paperclip. I counted out roughly sixteen hours of my net earnings, fastened the bills together, and set the money back in a pile that represented five weekly paychecks. I made similar judgments regarding the cash from the other shifts and then finally, with the whole day's deposits. I still wasn't used to seeing that much cash in one place, even if I had deposited a similar amount into the junk drawer of my trailer over the previous eighteen months. It was still a lot of money as far as I was concerned.

"And voila—I think I got it. I'm going to go over everything again before I let you check my work, but I'm pretty sure I got everything on the first try. I didn't think it would all come back to me from yesterday, but I remembered all of it. I didn't even need to look at my notes," said Lisa, obviously proud of herself.

"Alright. Just taking a quick glance at it, it looks like it all makes sense. You should put the cash in the bottom drawer if the office door is going to be open, though."

"Oh, I only had the door open for you. I'm going to count the cash again, and then I'll put it in a deposit bag in the bottom of the safe when I come out to finish up."

There was no reason for her to check her work, but I remembered wanting to do the same thing when Donna had trained me on the books. I needed to resolve the problem of my own uncertainty by measuring twice and cutting once, so it made sense that Lisa would do the same early on. I never felt comfortable enough to not seek out the tried and true to convince myself that I was on the right path, and I hadn't realized that most intelligent people weren't any more convinced of their own competence. As time passed, it became clear that the relative ease with which some seemed to go through life was borne out of a lack of investment rather than any sort of mastery. Lisa was wholly present and capable of everything I had thrown her way, though. I couldn't imagine that her day-to-day life was different any more than I could imagine myself going about mine without second-guessing every decision that I made. I found myself hoping that she would manage to escape the store as soon as possible, if not for her own sake, then because I knew that I was going to be outshined.

After Lisa finished up the books, we spent the rest of the shift cleaning the store from top to bottom and front to back. I had never worked with anyone willing to perform the job the way that I did, and I found the efficiency with which we managed to take care of things a bit unsettling. I had come to expect failure, and to see the culmination of all of my efforts realized so easily left me feeling empty. My struggles on all of those immaculate nights had—above all else—given me something upon which to focus. The accomplishment of the primary objective hadn't provided anything close to the sense of relief that I had imagined it would, and in the end, I was correct in my assumption that the only thing left to do was to start over from the beginning. There was no other option but to continue running through the playbook. By the time I made my way to the back room to grab the cleaning supplies for the bathroom, they were nowhere to be found. Lisa had already retrieved them and set off to do the job herself.

Chapter Twenty-Four

After our second day of training had come to a close, I knew that the circumstances dictated that Lisa should take care of the entire process of handing off to the next shift. She had a few more questions about the order of operations, but she hadn't forgotten to take care of any of the tasks that would ensure a proper shift change. The recent staffing turnover had all but guaranteed that our relief was either not going to be willing or not going to be able to meet Lisa halfway in that regard. Both attitude and aptitude had steeply declined throughout the remaining ranks outside of those of us with keys to the office. On this particular afternoon, we were treated to shift change with Joseph, whose shoddy work ethic and questionable dietary habits were rivaled only by his poor hygiene. He was competent on the register but wasn't good for doing anything else but standing there and complaining and smelling like a combination of sour milk and wet dog. I saw Lisa's nose wrinkle a bit when Joseph arrived for his shift, and I couldn't help but feel bad for her, knowing that she would have to take him into the office, shut the door, and talk to him about it for the first time within the next couple of weeks. She kept her disgust at bay and plastered on a cheerful and professional smile during their introductions, but I wondered if she would be able to do the same when she needed to drop to her knees to count cigarettes the first time she'd have to relieve him following an afternoon shift.

I was preoccupied with thoughts about my last conversation with Crystal. I hadn't thought that I'd said anything that wasn't true, but she hadn't been particularly receptive to what she'd likely viewed as having her faults pointed out. I hadn't felt any sort of kinship with her before that conversation, but I certainly did when I saw how quick she was to berate herself as if she had done something to deserve her poor treatment. I was no stranger to acting as my own worst critic and going so far as to make that perfectly clear to avoid anyone else feeling like they needed to offer up their own input. Up to that point, Crystal had seemed to be reasonably well put together for a young woman that had plainly made some pretty awful choices in life. She'd appeared to have such an easy time dealing with what was more than her fair share of bullshit, but that conversation made me see her in a different light. I found myself filling in some of the blanks of her backstory. It seemed that she had doubled down on her bad decisions so many times that a crash was inevitable. She'd built her life on a weak foundation, and our conversation gave me the feeling that she was more concerned with keeping up the appearance of that stability than anything else. This left her with no more compromises to make, and I think she had finally made the decision to go all in.

On this particular Sunday, changeover went off without a hitch. The store emptied in time for Lisa to run her shift report and based on how quickly she was catching on, I was pretty sure that we would be clocking out at 2:30 on the dot. I liked that. There wouldn't be any consequences for staying after the end of the shift, but I was always prouder than necessary when it came to adherence to the schedule. I was imagining that perfect column of zeros on my timecard when I heard the tell-tale beep that signaled that someone had recently finished fueling. Since Joseph had left the platform to get a fountain pop and Lisa had wisely chosen this moment as the best time to crouch down for her final safe drop, I was the only person with a clear shot at the parking lot. I glanced at the register and saw a pump number come up with an amount due, and I did what I had done dozens of times over the years: I bolted toward the door at a dead sprint. Based on past experiences, I knew that my split-second hesitation meant that I probably wouldn't be able the stop the driver of the vehicle. This did not matter in the slightest, though. What did—for reasons I'll never understand—was that I still made an effort in the face of those odds.

Drive-offs were a daily occurrence at the store. When they happened, we had to fill out a form with as much information as we could on both the perpetrator and the vehicle. We weren't expected to pay, but some of the cashiers did anyway. This always upset me, as not everyone had the available funds and those who did would pay before ever reporting anything—thus, looking like they were better at keeping their eyes on the pumps. Corporate would never have any reason to start requiring prepay if we didn't let them know just how bad it had become. Those were the days of surging fuel prices; gas was rarely below $2.50 per gallon, and it had spiked two dollars higher on several occasions. Some of the longer-tenured cashiers drove upwards of forty-five miles each way, and the idea of them paying for any more gas than they were already using was ridiculous. It was reprehensible that they should feel that their shitty jobs were in such danger that they needed to pay out of pocket for something that they had no way to prevent. If corporate actually cared about running the store well, they would have realized that they couldn't afford to lose good people over a problem with such an easy solution.

When Donna trained me, she'd told me that I should always try to stop vehicles from leaving the premises without paying.

The policemen who came out to take my drive-off reports reinforced that training, as they let us know that they didn't have the authority to hold people responsible for paying for gasoline when we continued giving them pre-approval to use the pumps. I was explicitly told that the local police did not have time to function as our company's loss prevention department. From time to time, they would escort drivers back to the station to pay, but that was the exception to the rule. It didn't take me long to understand that the law wouldn't be much help, and so I took it upon myself to do everything in my power to stop customers from driving off. I kept my head on a swivel and tried to take note of all of the people and vehicles at the pumps, and when I did see someone attempt to drive off, I would run out of the store with all of the grace that you might expect to see from a schoolgirl that happened to be engulfed in flames. For someone like Joseph—a morbidly obese smoker—what constituted making an effort looked much different. Most of the time, he barely made it off of the platform to shake his fist before the car was headed up the northbound ramp. Either way, we would each return to our posts behind the register, sweating and entirely out of breath.

While I got a good jump this time, I didn't see the vehicle pull away. I think that Joseph did his part in calling out the color, make, and model before I made it to the door, but the transfer of that information to my brain for processing and short-term storage was interrupted when I nearly put my head through an unexpected pane of glass. After moving the display cooler to the entryway to sweep, I'd forgotten that I had left the right-hand door's deadbolt engaged. My attempted burst through the doorway resulted in my bell being thoroughly rung, but I managed to spin around in time to exit through the other side and continue my pursuit. That wasn't the first time that I'd done that, but it was the first time it had ever happened in front of any of my coworkers. I immediately dreaded the fuss they would be making over me when I returned to the store. While I had probably suffered a mild concussion, I had more pressing concerns as I had no idea which vehicle I was chasing, or which exit they might be trying to take. I only knew that I needed to run toward the highway and hope that my all-out effort would once again suffice for acceptable performance of the task at hand.

As it turned out, the traffic on M-20 was such that I was able to catch up to the only vehicle leaving the parking lot. It was a silver Chrysler 300, and it featured a vanity plate that I was able to instantly commit to memory as I approached the tinted driver's side window:

VENAMUS

The trunk-rattling bass was loud enough that I figured that the driver hadn't heard me yelling all the way from the store to the sidewalk, and I briefly thought about tapping on the window to get his attention. It was probably for the best that I didn't need to.

"The fuck you doing, man? Y'all don't come up on me like that."

"I'm sorry, but I think you forgot to pay for your gas."

"The fuck I did. I got a receipt right here," said the driver, rummaging around the floorboards of the vehicle.

I waited nervously.

"You lucky you up here in the middle of nowhere. You try that shit where I'm from, and you never know. A'ight—I threw it out on the way out the store, man, but I ain't steal nothin'."

"That's fine, it should be on top of the trash, then."

"What the fuck, man… You think I'm gonna steal some gas? I don't know why you let people pump without paying anyway," said the driver.

"Well, the main office doesn't want people to think we're suspicious of our customers," I said, barely concealing my amusement.

"Man, this is crazy."

"Could I get you to pull up to the store so I can get you a receipt?"

"Shit, I don't want no trash receipt, man."

"I can actually print you a new one off the register, and we should be good."

"Nah, man. I ain't doin' that."

"Alright… I guess that's up to you, then.

I was still coming down as I watched the vehicle leave the parking lot and make a left turn, presumably to make his way toward the southbound ramp. I had the license plate and a description of the vehicle, but I knew from past experience that it still might not be enough for the police to take me seriously when I made the call. The fuel was gone, but I wasn't worried, as I felt that I'd made enough of a show that I was fundamentally beyond reproach. I was annoyed, but I didn't know what else I could have done to try to make the driver pay for his gas.

When I got back into the store, Joseph informed me that the pump had cleared off of the register just as I had made it out the door—the credit-card transaction had just taken longer to clear. That happened from time to time, but not enough to ever convince me not to do what I had done. With the drive-off a non-issue, Joseph made sure to make a far bigger deal of my head's meeting with the glass door than I would have liked. I've never been able to tolerate having attention called to my mistakes, regardless of the status of the person who does it. I spent enough of my waking time trying to forget my shortcomings and my inability to resolve them that it cut like a knife to have them pointed out to me. Joseph may have stunk like a forgotten bag of dirty gym shorts, but his combination of amusement and genuine concern made me just as angry as it would have coming from someone for whom I had a modicum of respect.

I still had a few minutes left in my shift, so I decided to head back to stock the cooler. Within a minute, I was already so busy filling empty slots and stacking crates and breaking down cardboard boxes that I didn't even notice that Lisa had followed me in to help out. I happened to glance in the direction of the door, and I saw her basically doing what amounted to checking my work, something that would have annoyed me in the past. I wasn't upset, as the years of being on edge had introduced a baseline level of aggravation directly into my consciousness. My inability to handle everyday stressors had led me to a sort of failed hypervigilance, where I spent so much time trying to recognize singular threats to stability that I couldn't help but miss most of them that came my way. I could identify the potential pain points, but I couldn't figure out how to feel like I had ever eliminated any of them, so I would just circle back and try again while reality ran roughshod over my best-laid plans. Lisa's presence should have been a calming influence, and I knew that her intentions were good, but I really felt defeated by her ease in dealing with all of the things that made my life so difficult. It was one thing to shrug everything off like most people, but I found it more impressive to see someone take it all as seriously as I did and somehow manage to smile about it.

Chapter Twenty-Five

With the cooler stocked and the paperwork finished, we were all but done for the day. As it was the last day of her training, it was Lisa's turn to make the deposit at the bank's twenty-four-hour drop box. I began to remind her of the intricacies of opening the safe, but she demonstrated that she had already taken care of it upon leaving the office. That was for the best, as I realized how much more condescending I sounded with every added detail. Lisa didn't seem to give it a second thought, as far as I could tell. However, Joseph's body odor was getting worse by the minute, and it's possible that she might just have been more focused on maintaining her intestinal fortitude when she dropped to her knees to retrieve the bag from the unlocked safe. Either way, I don't think she took offense—she wasn't the sort of person to do anything but outwardly express appreciation for any offered help.

I had established a policy of taking the money down to the bank every day that I did the books. While Donna had trained me to do it daily, my experience was that she would actually wait until Sunday to drop off the weekend's cash and checks. I knew that this was out of laziness, but I liked to imagine that it was actually the result of some solid reasoning. It could be argued that the more often people saw us going to the bank around the same time on the same days, the more likely we were to be robbed in the bank's unmonitored parking lot. However, I think a better way to look at Donna's actual methodology would be to apply the principle of Hanlon's razor;

although, sloth actually falls somewhere between malice and stupidity. In my case, I got a thrill from following arbitrary rules, especially when doing so pointed out the failure of others to follow suit. Without daily weekend deposits, we would be sitting on more than ten thousand dollars every Sunday, and that news was likely to spread to some questionable characters. I knew the kind of people we hired, and worse yet, I knew the sketchy sort of people that considered them to be trusted allies.

After clocking out, Lisa and I headed to our respective vehicles and made the short drive to the bank, with her taking the lead. I followed at a safe distance and noted that Lisa actually had a bit of a lead foot, which I hadn't expected. It was the first time that I had seen evidence that she was anything but a caricature of the person she presented herself to be. I wasn't comfortable sitting so high off of the ground while piloting Josh's old Blazer down Pickard, so I lagged behind. After a red light, I eventually made my way to the First Bank parking lot to find Lisa sitting in her Chevrolet Cobalt, listening to music and staring straight ahead into nothing while she waited for my arrival. I looked down from my perch and into her vehicle and saw that she had apparently taken my advice to heart, as the bank bag was not in plain sight. We rolled down our windows— her with the touch of a button and me with the use of a stripped mechanical crank requiring between two and three turns to complete a single gear's rotation. When the window was three-quarters of the way down, I decided that would be enough.

"So, yeah. You pretty much know what you're doing, right?" I asked.

"Yes. Turn the key to the left to open the door, put the bag inside with the zipper folded underneath so it doesn't catch, close the door, and turn the key two full rotations to the right to make it drop."

"Yeah, that's pretty much it."

"Pretty much? I don't think I forgot any steps..."

"Yeah, that's all there is. Nevermind me, I just don't like giving straight answers."

"Ah... okay... Oh, yeah—there is one more thing that you said."

"Yeah?"

"Yeah, you said to check it when I am done."

"Ah, yeah. Definitely do that. Definitely check it."

"Alright, will do. So, thank you for being so patient with me this weekend. I think I got it, but I guess we'll see next time, right?"

"Yeah, I guess so. I am in the office on Saturday, and you have Sunday, but I'll be there on the register."

"Can I still ask questions if I have any?"

"Of course. I don't think you're going to have any, though."

"Haha. We'll see about that."

"Alright. We should probably get moving here, just to be safe."

"Okay, cool. I'm ready to be home. Thanks again."

"You're welcome. Have a nice day, Lisa."

With that, Lisa made a picture-perfect, three-point turn and headed toward the night deposit box. I followed her while idly skipping through the radio stations and noting the differing decibel levels of the various white noise static that was made available for my consumption. I settled on the most pleasant unclear channel I could find and managed to faintly hear the last few bars of OutKast's "Hey Ya!" before someone tried to sell me something. It happened nearly every time I turned on the radio. I would always catch my song during the outro, and soon Tina Sawyer would further carve her way into my consciousness with another sales pitch masquerading as a fun giveaway. My college education had taught me that the music was just there to bridge the gaps between the advertisements, but the way that they were crowding the music out more and more with every month never did stop annoying me. I suppose that had a lot to do with why I never tried to do anything with my degree after I started at the store. There was a certain integrity in ripping people off directly to their faces, and there was a certain honesty in scrubbing toilets and mopping floors that I can't imagine selling advertising airtime or Two On The Town tickets or even vacuum cleaners could ever hope to match.

I looked up from the dial, steered the blue Blazer around the corner, and approached the deposit box just in time to see that Lisa had already pulled out of the parking lot. In a matter of a few seconds, I constructed an entertaining and elaborate scenario in which she was actually driving away with the money. After all, she had seemed to be overly concerned with discussing the bank bag throughout that morning's shift. After all, she had nervously sped down the road on her trip to the bank. After all, we couldn't be sure that her name was actually Lisa—it wasn't that hard to falsify documents, and management had often let people skate by without providing a Social Security number or references, until it was time to cut the first check, anyway. It would have been a pretty involved scam to run, from getting hired and trained and gaining trust and access, all for the chance to steal a few thousand dollars; but it was fun to think about.

After having whatever laugh there was to be had, I pulled forward to make sure that Lisa had actually done the double-check. I turned off the engine and took the keys out of the ignition a second before remembering that there was no reason for my work keys to be on Josh's key ring. I reached into my pocket, produced the correct set, and realized I was once again seated too high to reach the deposit box and I was once again parked too close to the building to squeeze in between to do it from the outside. I got back in the Blazer, moved it forward, turned off the engine, locked the doors, and walked back to the box. I stuck my key in the hole, made the necessary turn, and opened the container to reveal that Lisa had definitely not made off with the money. I was able to deduce that because the bank bag was still sitting right there in the container. The money was all still sitting right there in a thick maroon sack, separated out by shift, with perfectly completed deposit slips indicating just how much cash the store had brought in since the previous trip to the bank. It was all right there, waiting for anyone who might come across it, without a single camera to capture whatever might happen.

Chapter Twenty-Six

When I left the bank with the bag in tow, I was supposed to be headed to Josh's place to drop off the Blazer so that he could drive me back home. I went farther down Pickard Street to do that and was just about to make the left on Mission when I thought better of it and turned around. I wasn't headed back to the bank, but I wasn't headed back to my trailer, either. As easy as it would have been to make off with the cash, something in me told me that I shouldn't do that. I hadn't heard any sort of a still, small voice, though—I never really had much of a conscience anyway. My obsession with doing the right thing in the hardest way possible was more about keeping the eyes of judgment averted so that my transgressions and failures might be forgiven based on some unspoken credit system. This was different, though. I had done a lot of stupid things without giving much thought to the possible fallout, and I had no intention of putting a stop to that pattern. In this instance—rather than do what I should have or could have done—I made an executive decision.

The reality was that Logic Oil Company wasn't going to miss that money any more than the thousands of dollars in cash and merchandise that their employees and customers had stolen over the years. It stood to reason that the money that could have gone into paying a living wage was going into insurance against being ripped off by both their own lowlife staff and the general public. It was predictable. They promised competitive wages, which may sound appealing until you understand the concept of collusion. They advertised fair prices, but those prices were only as fair as they needed to be to not force the customer to realize just how much they had agreed to be screwed. It wouldn't have been difficult for me to justify stealing that deposit for myself and shrugging my shoulders if there had been any questions. Based on how the office had reacted when Paul made himself scarce, the likely outcome would be that they would fire Lisa for incompetence and the losses would be written off as part of the cost of doing business in the shitty way that they chose to do it.

I'd memorized Crystal's address the first time I paperclipped her check to her punch card. I had a knack for remembering that sort of minutia; in many cases, I would find a relationship between my thoughts and experiences with a person. With Crystal, the joke had always written itself. For as long as I had worked there, the address she had given was the old man's place, located at 6969 East Gladwin Road in Harrison Township. Gladwin was one of the biggest of the nothing-villages found in the vast wasteland just north of Clare, and the fact that the address was in Harrison lead me to believe that the road probably connected the two towns. It was most likely better known as a numbered state highway. With that in mind, I decided to drive north on US 127, take the first Harrison exit, and stop at a gas station to ask for directions. The drive was over thirty miles, so I had some time ahead of me to think about some things. I thought it best to try not to do too much of that. Instead, I focused my attention on a stolen half-pound of trail mix and a forty-four-ounce cup of free Diet Mountain Dew. I didn't have any of my CDs with me, and Josh had taken all of his out when we'd done the handoff, so I was stuck with the static once again. It didn't take me long to get through my improvised meal, and before long, there was nothing left to do but squint into the afternoon sun.

The truth was that I was more broken up about Crystal leaving the store than anything else, and I knew it. I didn't have much going on in my own life, and I didn't have any emotional stock in hers beyond how it affected the way that she treated me. The way I felt about her reminded me too much of how I felt about myself, with all of the focus directed at why I wasn't just another face along with the constant attempts to stay ignorant of all evidence to the contrary. I hated everyone because I hated myself, but with Crystal, I had been carrying out an experiment. I had purposely tried not to judge her as harshly as I judged myself. I had decided not to think of her in the way that I did the typical customer. I gave her the benefit of the doubt and allowed myself to consider her as a human being, something that I had done so little of in the past five years that I couldn't help but convince myself that she was something more. I hadn't felt that kind of meaning since the days of being ground into dust by a high school crush. Deserving or not, Crystal was the object of my affection, and by caring about her, I found it easier to care about myself. I wasn't sure if I deserved that.

I was not driving to Harrison to convince Crystal to ride back with me and start a new life. I didn't have visions of stepping in and being the good father that her kids never had or anything close to that. No part of me thought that I would show up with a bag of cash and my grand gesture would result in her falling in love with me; that wasn't my intent because, in the end, she just wasn't that special. She was a girl who had made some bad choices and had been doing a decent job of staying afloat despite her insistence on continuing down the same path. There were hundreds just like her in the Tri-Cities area, without even accounting for the others that played out the same script in every other nothing-county across the country. There were better-looking girls, smarter girls, and more interesting girls that were all playing that same part; for that reason, I suppose that I was lucky that I had only crossed paths with Crystal. All that aside, when I set off to drive to Harrison, I was actually doing it because it felt like the right thing to do. I was going to see a young woman who needed options, and I was going to hand her a bag full of them.

I was thinking about those options and my own lack of them when I finally took Exit 170 and was met with the choice of turning right or left. I considered ignoring the signs and taking the road less traveled, but I opted to stay the course and consult the nearest gas station attendant for further instruction. I remembered times when a customer would do the same at Pickard, asking me if they were headed in the right direction and somehow expecting a constructive answer despite a total lack of contextual clues about their point departure or final destination. I pulled into an old Citgo and pretended to check the prices on their trail mix before approaching the counter to ask the cashier if they could get me where I needed to go. The clerk gave me basic directions to head east on Gladwin Road, but cautioned that they were actually from Mount Pleasant and didn't know any addresses. I was informed that my best bet would be to pay attention to the mailboxes to find the right house number, which I told the cashier was something I had never before considered. I like to think they bought it, too. With only a vague sense of where I was and where I was headed, I set out for Casa Del Earnhardt.

While the middle of Michigan can't match the fresh coasts in terms of sheer beauty, there's something to be said for the vast amounts of nothingness to be explored in the north. It's not exactly remote, but it certainly lends itself to owning a four-wheel-drive vehicle and having easy access to a snowmobile. Even factoring in the dozens of villages that dot the landscape, it is mainly just a lot of trees and a lot of white guys in long johns, and not a whole lot else. You might see some farms and oil wells and perhaps other places of note, but there isn't much for the average young person to do but buy in or try to figure out how they're going to escape. Whenever I took a drive like the one I was taking on that day, my thoughts would wander in that direction. I would think about the sort of boredom that someone like myself would feel growing up in such an area, somehow forgetting that I had spent my teenage years in the middle of nowhere and had no problem dreaming up enough drama to make things seem worth caring about. There was no reason to think that Crystal had any trouble with that, and she had recently taken some solid steps to ensure that she wouldn't have to worry about it in the future either.

By the time I started heading east on M-61, I could feel my guts churning the way they always had back when I had things worth feeling anxious about. Regardless of whether the old man was home, there would be some sort of emotional stake involved at the end of my drive. I had driven out to the middle of nowhere to play white knight, with no second thoughts that I would get anything out of it other than the same non-existent, warm, fuzzy feeling that I had always never ended up feeling whenever I'd imagined that I had tried to do the right thing. I knew that if the old man were around, there would never be a better or worse time for me to give him a piece of my mind. I imagined landing the sort of stinging one-liners that always struck true and changed everything in the movies, but my experience told me that I shouldn't bet on that happening in real life. I would either be laughed at or I would face a physical confrontation for which I was definitely not ready. By the time the mailboxes started climbing into the six-thousands, I wondered if I would be better served by turning around and collecting my non-thoughts in the Citgo restroom before doing the smart thing and heading back to Mount Pleasant like nothing had ever happened.

It shouldn't come as any surprise that the farther you get away from civilization, the more privacy the average citizen craves. You might think that the one place where you would be comfortable with living at the front of your lot would be in the middle of nowhere, but for the most part, people out there want to have complete control over who and what they come into contact with every day. As a result, houses are few and far between and most feature long driveways obscured by dense tree coverage. You'll find an absurd amount of posted warnings regarding trespassing, as if there would ever be anything valuable enough inside to warrant a home invasion. It stood to reason that I was probably going to need to ignore one of those signs; the way my guts felt, I would need to invade the old man's bathroom before I could even focus on anything else. I was nervous. The whole thing began to seem more and more like a poorly thought out attempt at making a pointless gesture that was, at the very least, going to get me laughed at and quite possibly maimed. I slowed way down, not only to delay the inevitable but to better read the mailbox numbers so that I would pull in the correct driveway and thus be familiar with my eventual assailant.

I noticed that I was coming up to an intersection, where a sign told me that making a left would put me on Dodge Lake Road and a right would put me on Rogers Avenue. The way the numbers had recently jumped, I knew that I had to be getting close, but I didn't see any more houses. I did see a business with blacked out windows which didn't look promising. I glanced at the building's hand-painted address and realized that I had reached my destination. I saw no mailbox, no trees, and no long driveway. There wasn't even a house. However, a sign out front made it clear that not only was the old man not there, but there probably wouldn't be anyone around until sometime after 5:00 PM. I had a bit of a wait on my hands, but it was just as well. I didn't have anything better to do than see the whole thing through. With that thought in mind, I parked the car and glanced at the sign one more time. The sign in front of 6969 East Gladwin Road in Harrison, Michigan read:

SHOWGIRLS
MICELI'S CORNER
OPEN WED-SUN 5 PM
NOW HIRING CLASS OF 2007

ABOUT THE AUTHOR

Mark Hunter lives in Indianapolis, Indiana with his wife, their dog, and their cat. When he isn't working the night shift, he is usually listening to music or reading about baseball or playing the guitar. Every once in a while, he tries to write something, and he's very sorry about that. Mark Hunter is also the author of *Middle Seconds*.

Please feel free to reach out to Mark at:
markhunter21279@gmail.com
Facebook: markhunternovelist
Twitter: markhunterindy
Instagram: markhunter21279

Made in the USA
Middletown, DE
14 February 2022

61112475R00125